REA

JUL 1 4 2005

SWEET LUCY WINE

ALSO BY DABNEY STUART

POETRY

The Diving Bell (1966)
A Particular Place (1969)
The Other Hand (1974)
Round and Round: A Triptych (1977)
Rockbridge Poems (1981)
Common Ground (1982)
Don't Look Back (1987)
Narcissus Dreaming (1990)

FOR CHILDREN

Friends of Yours, Friends of Mine (1974)

CRITICISM

Nabokov: The Dimensions of Parody (1978)

SWEET LUCY WINE

STORIES BY
DABNEY STUART

LOUISIANA
STATE
UNIVERSITY
PRESS

BATON ROUGE
AND
LONDON

1992

First printing
01 00 99 98 97 96   95   94   93   92   5   4   3   2   1
Designer: Glynnis Phoebe
Typeface: Sabon
Typesetter: G & S Typesetters, Inc.
Printer and binder: Thomson-Shore, Inc.

Library of Congress Cataloging-in-Publication Data
Stuart, Dabney, 1937–
    Sweet Lucy wine : stories / by Dabney Stuart.
       p.   cm.
    ISBN 0-8071-1707-2 (cloth)
       I. Title.
    PS3569.T8S94   1992
    813'.54—dc20   91-21245
                                                             CIP

The author is grateful to Washington and Lee University for two John M. Glenn
grants, which were helpful during the composition of these stories.

The stories in this collection were originally published, often in different form,
as follows: "Anders" as "Bobby Cross" in the *Xavier Review*, Vol. VIII, Nos.
1–2 (1988); "Tidewater" in the *Crescent Review*, Vol. I, No. 2 (1983); "Luke"
as "Meat" in *Pembroke Magazine*, No. 23 (1991); "Sweet Lucy Wine" as
"Lord Jack and Wonderbuns" in the *Chattahoochee Review*, Vol. VI, No. 2
(Winter, 1986)—the first section of the story having first appeared as "Sweet
Lucy Wine" in the *Ohio Review*, No. 26 (July, 1981); "Mr. Mann" in *Epoch*,
Vol. XXXIV, No. 1 (1984–85); parts of "Rafer McBride" as "Tater McBride's
Chair" in *Cottonwood Magazine*, No. 36 (Fall, 1985), as "Tater McBride's
Girls" in the *Richmond Quarterly*, Vol. IX, No. 2 (Fall, 1986), and as "Playing
Touch" in *Crosscurrents*, Vol. IV, No. 4/Vol. V, No. 1 (Spring, 1985); "Straw-
berry Hill" in the *Chattahoochee Review*, Vol. X, No. 4 (Summer, 1990);
"Homespun" in *Negative Capability*, Vol. IX, No. 3 (March, 1991); "DuPo" in
the *Texas Review*, Vol. V, Nos. 1–2 (Spring/Summer, 1984); "Easy" in the
Montana Review, No. 5 (1984).

for Sandra
and for my children: Martha, Nathan, and Darren

CONTENTS

SWEET LUCY WINE

EASY

SWEET LUCY WINE

ANDERS

Mark Random started second grade when his little brother Luke was only a year old, but to Random it seemed as if the time they had had him had been just one long day and night.

Random remembered his coming home at first, almost too small to hold in your hand; he had watched Luke getting cooed over, and then becoming king of the crib and playpen after that. Jack Armstrong and Hop Harrigan and the Little Shepherd, he had come to think, rolled into one round ball of look-at-me-forever.

Random understood he was supposed to let Luke be, so he let him be. But it all seemed an excruciating day and night anyway—and then the next morning, like the second day in the Bible, for his reward he got to go back to school.

For the first three or four months he rode in a car with his cousins. Some days when he left he would pass Luke lying in his pen sucking his feet, or in his high chair smearing his food into his face. Luke always looked at him with the same sappyassed blankness when he went by. Once Luke pulled himself up by the bars on the playpen and was pushing himself up and down on his toes, singing some baby nonsense. When Random looked in at him he stopped singing, and Random could have sworn he poked his tongue out at him. Probably just licking his splotchy cheeks, he thought, but all the same.

His energy had seemed to run suddenly to his right leg and he felt himself want to cut loose and kick an all-time record field goal with that roly-poly body. Bang, end-over-end, cleanest follow-through in the history of little brothers.

He'd come home and it would be the same, as if he'd never left; he felt as if what he did all day wasn't real, that only Luke lying around doing nothing but being waited on and worshiped like a little idol was.

When Random got used to going to school, which if pressed he would have to admit he never really did, he started leaving home earlier, and walking. He still had to put up with Luke, but less, and some days Luke would still be asleep when Random left. It went on that way for a couple of years, until the pen and high-chair periods were over and Luke was being treated like an all-American because he could dress himself and do other miraculous stuff like that.

By the time Random hit sixth grade he had developed the pattern of leaving the house before his father had gotten up to get ready to go to work.

It didn't seem to matter no one else was at school when he got there, usually around seven fifteen or seven thirty. Sometimes he would beat the janitor, Mr. O'Neill, and have to wait outside the heavy double doors to the big hall between the two playgrounds. He would make a pipe with his hands against one of the windows and press his face into it next to the glass.

It was pretty dark in there, but his eyes became used to it inside his hands, and soon Mr. O'Neill would rise up at the top of the basement steps carrying the softball and bat. Random would back up and Mr. O'Neill would open one of the doors and hand the equipment to him.

"Gonna play with yourself again?" the old man would say. He never really looked at Random, just out the door toward the tennis courts and nobody.

Before Random could answer him the door would be oozing shut, Mr. O'Neill disappearing down the stairs, taking off his coat, going to work in the dim recesses of the basement where Random was sure no one else ever went.

Until about a quarter to eight he would be on the courts hitting line drives into the tall chain link fence, liking that rattling sound almost as much as the feeling of the bat on the ball. In the newsreel one Saturday he had been stunned to see, in slow motion, how the ball flattened when it hit the bat, and he imagined that happening when he swung. He would feel the flatness in his wrists and all the way up his arms into his shoulders. Sometimes his own muscles seemed to be making the shimmying sound of the fence when the ball hit it.

He didn't hit home runs, but he still felt exhilarated, as if he were winning something.

Carl Peters would usually show up first. He and Random would hit flies to each other until enough people accumulated for work-up, which they would play until the bell summoned them inside. Danny Streater, always jerking his blond hair off his forehead, would be there, and Charles Homan, who thought the girls were always watching him. Danny and Charles and Random would dominate the bat because they knew the technique of hitting line drives against the fence off any kind of pitching. As long as one drove the ball into the fence, no one could catch it.

Sometimes when Random was swinging two or three extra bats on deck, or had popped up and was in the field, he would notice Bobby Anders standing over on the side by the hedge in right field. He always stood in foul territory, Random noticed, as if he wasn't really playing, and he always had a stupid grin on his face, just standing there, glasses on, hands in his pockets. Sometimes he wore short pants to school.

By the time the bell rang there would be so many people on those two tennis courts Random thought you could've driven them to market. It seemed strange to him that such a crowd could gather so soon after he had been alone, as if he never had been, or had dreamed he was, or there wasn't all that much difference, except for the noise.

Inside, school was school. He did well enough, but he hated it. Everybody did, he guessed, but he didn't hear them carry on too much about it in the open. He would sit there where he was supposed to and mostly do what the teacher said, even going to the special rooms set aside for art and singing once a week.

He didn't mind art so much, but the woman who came to teach music acted odd, as if she put on the person she was, like clothes, and paraded it in front of the students. Her tone of voice reminded him of his mother's when she was on the phone planning garden club meetings. The music teacher spoke of "freeing up the diaphragm" and "pitch" as if their survival depended on mastering it all. Random would watch as she poked out her round chest, stuck a little flying saucer in her mouth, and blew on it. A buzzy hum would come out, which she expected them to imitate; Random never could, much less sing afterwards. Shit, he would mutter to himself, not understanding how anybody could get from the thick insect noise to music, even though he heard some people do it, including Bobby Anders.

Recess offered a way out, but Random had to admit it wasn't really all that hot. When it rained, which sometimes seemed every day, they were herded downstairs, all the way underground, boys to the boys' basement, girls to the girls', to kill the same time in a smaller space. The windows were in a line at the top of the walls. He could see the bottom of the outdoor water fountain, and Mr. O'Neill's feet if he went by in his raincoat.

All he could remember doing down there was wrestling on the mats. They weren't regular matches, when two people hunch over like apes and circle around and pounce on each other with a referee. Random decided the best way to describe it was, they made piles. Five, eight, ten people, maybe more—nobody really counted—they would climb over each other, wrought up, tangled, wrapped in crazy shapes. Half the time no one could tell which arms and legs and shoulders belonged to who.

The object was to keep from getting squshed on the bottom, so all the movement, some of it desperate, tended to be upwards, like worms trying to wiggle out of the ground. There was a lot of leg clipping and rolling to the side, and if someone got trapped underneath, his nose and mouth were mashed against the mat, which was dusty and full of little grains like sand, but not sand. No one could figure out how they got there, but the unlucky boys would end up with them stuck in their cheeks or necks like caraway seeds in cheese.

Random's experience had taught him that everybody got smushed into the mat sometimes. Whenever he found himself down there feeling all those squirming people trying to push him through the grusty canvas and the cement floor, somehow he always saw Bobby Anders sitting across from the mats on one of the wall benches fiddling with a key chain, or leaning against one of the sinks between the doors to the toilets. Half-smiling at Random, or looking past him lying there with his head twisted sideways, or backwards, or off, feeling as if he'd just as well be dead. To Random it was always the same dumb smile, and it seemed to him an appropriate accompaniment to the condition he was in down there on the mat.

When the weather was good the students would come bursting out of the big blue double doors all at once, calling to each other what they were going to do, and then everyone would spread out over the playground. They played tag, boys-chase-the-girls (or vice versa), some kind of ball; they swung on the swings, maneuvered on the monkey bars, shot marbles. *Nobody did nothing.*

This was the routine. It happened often, especially in the spring, and although Random was an unexceptional part of it, when he remembered these years it seemed to him as if there had been only one day, the day he finally got tired of Bobby Anders.

Everything had proceeded in its ordinary way until after lunch. Danny Streater and Random went to the skinned ground under the oak trees to shoot marbles until the fifth-period bell. Danny was on a streak, five or six creamies up, to Random's dismay. Danny set up a favorable angle across from Random, walked over and knuckled down, aiming at his next target. His floppy hair fanned downwards, catching sunlight in a line on its edge.

Random looked past that glinting just before Danny shot and saw Bobby Anders leaning on one of the support bars at the end of the swing set. He saw dark blobs shifting back and forth in the air behind Bobby Anders, with his body frozen sharply in front. It reminded Random of the shots in the movies when the camera focused suddenly on something the character hasn't ever quite seen that way before, an instant of clarity.

Only Random wasn't seeing anything new. Just Bobby Anders, he thought, same old shit-eating grin. Random had the strange idea that Bobby Anders probably always got what he wanted for dinner without asking for it, probably never had to eat eggplant or turnip greens. He was just standing there, one elbow propped on the cross bar, his whole body aimed into his lowtops as if nothing would ever get in between any of it. The sun hit his glasses so they became blank with light. Random couldn't tell what he was looking at, if he was looking at anything.

Danny Streater pushed himself up on his knees, cussing. "Hand me my shooter, Random," he said. Random couldn't remember if he did or not. The next thing he knew he was screaming incomprehensible words at Bobby Anders, pushing him against the chest, backing him up past the tetherball pole until they were facing each other on the tennis courts.

As Random remembered it, what he yelled had mostly to do with how tired he was of Bobby Anders hanging around, never doing anything, always watching, somehow making Random feel as if part of himself wasn't where he was, or doing what the rest of him was doing, as if, simply because of Bobby Anders' presence, he was split in two parts, each of which was a stranger to the other. Bobby Anders left his glasses on and Random thought his freckles were bigger next to his eyes than on the rest of his face.

Random had had fights before, fairly often to be honest about it. He had poked Barry Gamble in the eye badly enough to get hauled into the principal's office two weeks earlier, and he and Melvin Berley tangled sometimes, it seemed to him, almost for fun. Random thought Berley was a shitass with a mean temper, which was probably true, and he enjoyed fighting him. In fact, he enjoyed fighting, period—it seemed part of what he had been sent to school to do, since there was a standing prohibition against it at home.

But this time it felt different, more confusing. It wasn't that he didn't want to hit him. He did. He wanted the crunched-up pieces of Bobby Anders' glasses to jam into his eyes and cheeks. Wanted to feel Bobby Anders' face sqush under his fist and his brains come gushing out like oatmeal. He wanted all that. Wanted Bobby Anders lying on the asphalt sniveling and whimpering like a kicked puppydog, or a baby nobody would pick up.

But, at the same time, he didn't want to hit him either; it was as if Bobby Anders' face was there in front of him, like an ocean. Or, Random felt, it would grow into an ocean and swallow him if he didn't slug it. Random felt that the sooner he plunged his fist into Bobby Anders' face the less chance that his arm and then his whole body would follow and be drowned inside Bobby Anders forever.

The longer Random waited the more frightened he became. Even then, however, he was aware that being scared made him want to hit Bobby Anders harder. But hitting him harder, ramming his fist clean through his face and out the back of his head, meant going deeper into him, which was what he was scared of.

He never thought about hurting himself, never thought about pieces of Bobby Anders' glasses getting stuck in his fingers, or his knuckles and hand getting bruised, or maybe broken. He thought of none of that, much less about being beaten. He just saw ahead, as if what he wanted was going to be what was.

So he swung. He didn't take a stance, or crouch, or wind up, or anything. Just lapped his right arm out like a snake striking. And he had the odd sensation, too, that Bobby Anders' face zoomed up toward his fist.

He heard a dull smack, and saw Bobby Anders' glasses follow his hand off the side of Bobby Anders' head. He watched them fall to the ground. He noticed his own arm hanging limp beside him, all by itself, and wondered *How'd that get there,* as if it wasn't his arm at all.

Bobby Anders' face looked naked, as people's faces always seemed to Random when suddenly he saw them without their glasses. He always wanted to protect them. Bobby Anders had two little flecks of blood beside his eye, and his left hand was on the way to feel his cheek. One of his friends moved toward him in the background, like a shadow.

He bent down and picked up his glasses, and it was all over. Random knew immediately that it was the most unsatisfying fight he'd ever picked. It hadn't resolved a thing. Bobby Anders just walked off toward the water fountain, studying his glasses, a bunch of people gathered around him, talking, asking questions Random couldn't quite hear.

Random stood there and stared at him. Anders shook his head once, as if he were getting water off his face from swimming. Random saw his red hair flick down on his forehead, and back up.

Then he disappeared around the side of the building and Random was left standing in the courts by himself. It struck him even then as profoundly odd—that same way his fear had struck him—but he wanted to be holding something, he didn't know what—a big block, a bagful of laundry, a body—anything big and hefty so he could carry it in both arms, hug it to himself, and not be only one person standing there, befuddled, with nothing to go on.

And he knew it would have even been okay if Bobby Anders had come back. He could have just walked up, not as if nothing had happened but as if everything had, and Random could take him in his arms and it would be all right, not again, but maybe for the first time.

But he didn't. He was gone. The bell rang soon after and Random went back into the building to more school. Halfway up to the room he heard the heavy door with the exit bar slam shut at the bottom of the stairwell.

TIDEWATER

Odd as it seems, Mark Random remembered it as the day his brother Luke caught the rubber.

They were down in front of their grandfather's house, fishing with poles he had made them of broomsticks, string, and bent pins. They would lie down on the flat top of the cement breakwater, lean over the edge, and pick off the little snails stuck there below the tide line. Then they would crack open the shells and put the insides on the pins for bait.

All they caught were minnows. Some of them were fairly fat, however, and when they grabbed the snails and tried to run off with them they tugged the pole hard enough to be exciting. Random knew nobody would fall off the breakwater because of it, but it was still a pretty fair pull.

Since Random and Luke had no reels, they simply jerked back and the minnow would come flying out of the water. If it held onto the snail long enough it would sail over their heads and land in the grass behind them, whapping and flopping until they got it back into the water.

Doing that was sometimes harder than getting them out, they were so slippery and quick. Random enjoyed chasing them in the grass. When he caught them, though, he couldn't hold them gently because they flapped through between his fingers, and he couldn't hold them tight because they squirted out of his hands like water from a water pistol.

For all that to happen the tide had to be up. When it was low, about fifteen feet of muck opened up between the yard and the edge of the receded water. And there was another thirty-five feet of water before it got deep enough at the boathouse at the end of the dock for Random's grandfather to moor his boat.

Broken shells and cans and bits of trash stuck in pieces up out of the muck. Hunks of torn cloth that after a few hours in the sun would dry out and turn gray. Caved-in old tires that reminded Random of his uncle Seldom's toothless mouth, except for the slick green scum that covered them. Here and there a dead white crab claw or shell.

Random expected something that white stuck in something as black as the sludge would shine when the sun hit it. But it didn't. It just looked dead, as did the million barnacles on the dock posts, which also disappeared when the tide came in.

All that, and rubbers.

Random's mother had told him once they were balloons. He never decided whether she was just handing herself the usual shit about his being too young to understand, or whether she really didn't know. With her drawn-up mouth and straight shoulders, Random thought you could go either way and give odds, because she hated grunge and regular smells and stickiness and such, and the rubbers had all that and more, no matter what you called them.

Random had perpetuated the lie by telling Luke that's what they were, balloons. When the tide was ebbing but hadn't finished, or was just starting to come in, they would float in the low water, usually one or two, but sometimes more. Once Random counted thirteen of them clustered in front of the breakwater, like a little school of fish.

On this particular day, though, there was only one, and as they stood on the breakwater watching it float back and forth in the shallow rivulets Luke had decided to catch it and blow it up.

"You gonna put your mouth on that thing?" Random asked him.

"Why not?" Luke said, as if it was as natural as eating a strawberry. "You didn't think of it."

"Neither did my ass," Random said.

"I can't help it if you got a dumb ass," Luke said, turning away and starting up the yard to get his pole.

Since it was in the garage way around back of their grandparents' big house, Random knew that would take a while, so he walked along the breakwater to the dock. Besides that, he wanted to get his mind off the sleazy rubber, which he didn't need to know was a rubber to be disgusted by the prospect of his brother's blowing on it. The water and what he could see on the bottom when the tide was out was enough to make him sick; how anyone could consider getting intimate with an object that had been floating in it God knows how long, he couldn't understand. He spat into the water. A minnow surfaced and pecked at the white blob until it disappeared.

Random started walking out the dock, fitting his bare feet at angles to the boards. Most of them were thin so he had to splay almost completely slue-footed, but every now and then one would be wide enough to take his whole foot straight on.

His trying not to step on the cracks between the boards, and staring down at the wavery sparkles on the water, had nearly hypnotized him when he reached the boathouse, so he stopped for a minute and then walked normally around the boathouse porch, past his grandfather's boat where the old man was working on the engine, and on to the end of the dock beyond it.

Willy Tidewater was sitting out there fishing. "Real fishing," Random called it, to differentiate it from the minnow fishing he did off the breakwater.

"How you doin'?" Random asked him, standing so his shadow fell across Tidewater's hands.

"You doan wanna know," he said, without turning around. The sun seemed to hit the water at the exact spot where his line dove into it, and the water moved enough to make the sunspot and the line's reflection wiggle, like worms.

"Yeah I do," Random said. "But you don't have anything to show me."

Sometimes when Willy wasn't catching anything and was bored he would bait Random, but this time he reached out with his left hand and shifted the cover on his bucket so Random could look in.

Random saw nothing at first, his eyes needing time to adjust. Then a movement in the water made a miniature whirlpool in the middle of the bucket. When it stopped, Random saw an eel coiling against the sides, disappearing into the bottom. It was about as thick as Random's arm and only a little darker than the water.

"It's another one underneath of him," Willy Tidewater said. He turned his head toward Random and his teeth shone in his black face like another sunspot. "How you feel?" he asked, and chuckled in his throat. "Want me to hold 'em up fo you? They's coilers, real nice, slide all over theyselves."

He ran the heel of his hand up under his nose and Random turned and went through the screen door onto the boathouse porch.

Willy Tidewater knew what eels did to Random's stomach. Random had watched him tear out the rotting wooden breakwater a year before to put in the cement replacement, and he'd seen Random throw up when he started hauling out the eels that had gotten trapped behind the boards when the tide went out. There were at least twenty of them.

"Told you," he said over his shoulder, chuckling again. "You learn to believe ole Willy one day." He was the only person who didn't call himself Tidewater. "Ain't my name," he'd say, "and doan ax me what is, neither."

Random felt a little better getting out of the sun and sitting down. He leaned up against the boathouse wall and watched Willy Tidewater catch a couple of spot. About the time Random's queasiness over the eels had subsided he heard Tidewater cuss. He stood up and watched him drag a mud toad out of the water. It splatted around on the dock near the bucket.

Willy Tidewater laid down his rod. With his knife in his right hand he crawled over to the mud toad. "Godawful ugly excuse for a fish," he said. "Motherless bastids." The only way to unhook one of them was to stab it in the back first and then go in after the hook with a pair of pliers.

"Shit," Willy Tidewater said, trying to get a grip on the mud toad. Random wanted to watch everything but because he knew what it would do to him he walked over to the other end of the L-shaped porch and stood looking over the water toward the yard. He could tell from the change on the breakwater that the tide was coming in.

As he saw Luke ambling down the yard carrying his pole, he heard the sputous gurgling noise the mud toad made as Willy Tidewater drove his knife in.

"You hokey-toed idiot," he yelled through the screen at Luke. Then he went through the door back onto the corner of the dock where his grandfather's boat was tied. "You put your mouth on that thing and you'll die for a week."

Luke didn't even look at him. He sat down on the breakwater and started unwinding the string off his pole. The way it stuck up in the air made Random think he could have put a flag on the end of it and marched in a Fourth of July parade. He felt a sudden urge to grab Willy Tidewater's knife and go up there and cut the thing into little pieces like a trash fish for bait.

Random unstuck a blob of dried birdshit from a dock board with his toe and nudged it through a crack. When he turned and walked over to the edge of his grandfather's boat, Willy Tidewater heaved the mud toad high out into the deeper water. Random watched it arc end-over-end through the air, and splash, and saw Willy Tidewater wipe his hands on his overalls and sit down to rebait his hook.

"Nice arm," Random yelled to him.

Tidewater squeezed a look over his shoulder at Random, the sunlight catching in the sweat on his face. "Ain't no game," he said.

Random couldn't hear how he said it, just the words, but he was sure Tidewater was digging at him because he hadn't hung around after he saw the eels. Tidewater turned back to his fishing.

Random stared at him for a couple of seconds, seeing nothing unusual, just the sun dazzling the water in a line out from the dock. Watching it, he was aware of a dull heaviness forming in his eyes. He turned his head toward Luke in the yard. What's the little sumbitch doing now? he thought. He was concentrating on Luke leaning over the breakwater dangling his line in the shallows, probably trying to hook the rubber, his nose and eyes and mouth scrunched together in the middle of his face, when Random felt something grab his ankles.

It felt as if a vise had clamped on each one; he half expected a sea monster to use them as posts to help pull itself out of the creek. He had a feeling that seemed not so much fear as the attempt to avoid fear; he saw himself, as if from a distance, being lifted high into the air, and shot, arching, into the water, like Willy Tidewater's mud toad. He felt himself floating in the sky already as he watched, not really watching.

It didn't happen, of course. The hands massaged his ankles affectionately, and then squeezed them, a substitute hug.

It was his grandfather. He was standing in the stern of the boat, reaching over the edge of the dock. He smiled at Random, the big, accepting smile Random had come to depend on even though he realized it never quite matched the expression in his grandfather's eyes, which looked darker, as if partly submerged; but the two seemed closest when he was on his boat.

Random smiled, too, knowing his grandfather knew he'd scared him. Neither of them minded. Half the floor that covered the engines was raised and Random could see the black, greasy shaft of one of them in the hold behind his grandfather. His face had some oily smears, and when he took his hands off Random's legs they left smudges.

He didn't say anything, but turned around and walked over to the engine. He grunted as he lowered himself in beside it and rattled a wrench out of the tool box.

Random went to the bow, curling his big toes under as he walked, and sat down on the edge of the dock. He began to push the edge of the boat with his feet. It would ease out to the end of the tieline, the line would stretch and creak, and then the boat would slowly drift back in toward him. He developed a lazy, predictable rhythm between his leg and the boat.

What happened next, however, in the middle of what he would have called a *monovating* routine, would be hard for him to describe.

He had taken his eyes off the boat to look at his brother. Luke had hauled something—probably the rubber, Random thought— out of the water, very carefully, as if it were an egg that would break if he dropped it. When he got it over the breakwater he swung it up into the yard.

At the time Luke dropped his pole and started to bend down toward the rubber in the grass Random noticed, out of the side of his eye, that his foot was reaching out for the edge of the boat to give it an outward push, only there was no boat where his leg expected it to be. He also noticed that the foot he saw didn't seem to be his foot. He felt as if he were nowhere, not really watching himself, or, indeed, anything.

His butt slipped off the edge of the dock and he fell into the water.

He could swim, but he didn't. At any rate not the kind of swimming you'd expect under the circumstances. He moved more like a fish or a seal than a human being. Under water. He saw himself breaststroking and wriggling and squirming, as if he'd been trapped in a tube just big enough to move his arms in.

It was as if the memory of the experience and the experience itself were happening at the same time.

The water didn't seem to him all the same dark green color most of it was. He finned past some green-lighted patches, and the air bubbles from his nose looped by him like paper birthday chains. He neared one of the dock posts and seemed to study the barnacles closely, as if they were a map of where he should go next.

But he never tried to crawl up to the surface and swim in to the shallows where he could stand up. Those barnacles were the last thing he remembered. Everything finally merged into the same color when he had filled his lungs with water.

Black.

Zero.

The next thing he knows he is still doing the sidewinding breaststroke, imitating an eel, only this time he is in his grandfather's arms like a baby; he's already been carried down most of the dock and is about ten feet from the breakwater and the yard.

He is flailing and thrashing and can't understand why his shirt is soaking wet. The only noises he hears are groans and vomiting sounds, which he is too disoriented to realize are his own. Inside his head he's screaming at his grandfather to leave me be, put me back, let me find out for myself about being a fish, can't you see I'm breathing okay, it's none of your business anyhow what I do with my life, all you other guys with your heads in your engines and buckets and privates, what do you know about how it is under water?

Except, of course, he spoke none of that out loud. He was too busy spitting up and moaning.

Then, inexplicably, he stopped, relaxing in his grandfather's arms like a beaten fish, his head hanging loosely, his calves flopping down over the old man's arm. He felt his grandfather's surprise when he stopped thrashing; he almost dropped Random, but made a hitching movement and got a better grip on him.

Since Random was lying on his back, the next series of perceptions came to him upside down. Even if he had been rightside-up, however, seeing the world as he was used to seeing it, there's no certainty anything would have been any clearer.

His mother was squatting beside Luke in the grass. Or she was rising up out of a squat. On her face he recognized a version of her *Oh-that's-vile* expression, as if it wanted to fade but couldn't.

Luke was sitting cross-legged, one arm down beside him rubbing the grass the way one rubs a place on his body after bumping into something, the other arm folded up in the air, wavering. His face was screwed up with crying; the way Random was looking at it made it resemble a grimace, reminding him of the faces of humpbacked statues he had seen on the roofs in photographs of serious buildings.

His mother rose up. A stunned yelp escaped her mouth. She ran toward Random a few steps and then stopped, leaned forward, and leaned back. One hand flew up into her mouth. For an instant Random was sure she was going to eat her hand.

Her vile expression strengthened again, and then a frightened one replaced it, and then something Random didn't recognize, or want to: a kind of erasing look, saying that if she could have made everything vanish—Luke's gurgling in the grass, Random and her father soggy with creek water and greasy from the engines in the boat—she would have.

Her eyes flattened and it seemed to Random that in another second they would flake off and blow away.

His grandfather put him down then, and she moved as if to come toward Random and put her hands on him.

He turned and ran up the ragged flagstones toward the house, not knowing what else to do, in fact having already done everything he could think of, and the high windows and the long porch seemed deeper than he'd ever seen them, leaning down as if to engulf him.

It didn't seem to matter to him that until now the house had always presented itself as a friendly place. All he could think was *I've had a bellyful of that.*

When he reached the steps he swung left onto the sidewalk that ran in front of the porch. He followed it out to its end, little bright jags like lightning going up from his neck into the base of his head each time one of his feet slapped against the cement.

At the gate he stopped and let his thumb rest on the lever of the latch. It felt sticky, as if the new paint hadn't quite dried. He pushed down and opened the gate and took a few steps out into the graveled lane at the dead end of which his grandfather's house stood.

He held on to the open gate and looked down the lane. It wasn't anything it hadn't always been, but for the first time Random saw how it went straight out of there from the place he stood, and a block away where it met Broad Street the trees stopped brooding over it and sunlight was pouring down on everything.

LUKE

Mr. Wendle was having his eleven o'clock hawk.

Although it might sound as if Mark Random observed this ritual every day, he was actually present for it only on Saturdays. He and Luke came to their father's place of business, a wholesale hardware office and warehouse combination, every Saturday.

Their father worked half a day each weekend. Random always figured he and Luke got to come along so their mother could have a morning off from them. She had been the one who convinced them it was what they wanted to do in the first place. She had made it sound like a birthday party, staying up late, and (for Luke, Random thought) eating boogers all rolled into one. In fact, Random realized that Saturday mornings were the only time they were allowed to get really dirty without her throwing a conniption about it.

The procedure didn't bother him particularly, not even when he got older and other ways to spend Saturday mornings began to present themselves, but being there became boring after an hour or so. Sliding down the metal freight chute from the top floor got to be old real quick. That's probably why they made sure they were in the left-hand men's room at eleven, when Mr. Wendle went into the one next door to have his hawk.

There weren't any ceilings over the men's toilet cubicles, so Random climbed up on the sink as he usually did, his feet braced against the inside of its front, the rest of him leaning toward the wall with his hands curled over the top of the partition for support. He imagined if anybody ever saw him from the other side he would look like Kilroy.

When Mr. Wendle came in, Luke started to pull on Random's pants leg to get him to show what Mr. Wendle was doing. Random always repeated Mr. Wendle's moves in pantomime, so Luke could imagine what went with the sounds.

No one had any trouble hearing the sounds.

Once Baker Bridewater had slid down the spiral metal chute all the way from the sixth floor because he thought someone was dying. He had been recently hired as a stockman and didn't know about Mr. Wendle's hawks.

Random remembered the incident. He and Luke had been on the chute on the third floor arguing about who was going first the next time down when they heard Bridewater above them, hollering to beat hell.

"Clear the chute! Clear the chute!"

They could hear Mr. Wendle's hawking and Bridewater's yelling, first one and then the other, and then the sound of Baker thumping onto the chute and starting down.

They climbed over the edge onto the floor, pulling out the flattened cartons they used for higher speed just as Bridewater came sliding by. He wasn't using a carton, but he was helping himself along by grabbing the sides of the chute and pulling. He looked to Random like a man rowing a boat without any oars. He was moving pretty good, too.

Random had wondered if Bridewater had come off at the bottom standing up. The last stretch of chute, about fifteen feet, shines like the moon's trail on still water and is slicker than the toilet paper at the bus station. If one wasn't experienced he could spill over if he came off sitting down. Standing up was worse. He had come down standing up only twice himself, and one of those times he had lost his balance and pitched over into the excelsior bin.

He and Luke had hopped in again as soon as Bridewater had gone by. They missed seeing him come off the chute, but were just outside the right-hand men's room door when he broke in and got his introduction to Mr. Wendle.

Some introduction, Random thought.

Just as Bridewater threw the door open Mr. Wendle let loose a large, green lump into the sink. There was nothing for Bridewater to do but stare for a couple seconds, and then let his breakfast loop up into the commode behind Mr. Wendle.

Mr. Wendle had gone right on with his hawking. He had hawked all the way through World War II and both floods that had drowned the drums of kerosene and linseed oil and turpentine in the warehouse basement, so nothing Baker Bridewater could have dreamed up for his breakfast was going to interrupt him now.

He paid no attention to Luke and Random, either, but Bridewater's yelling and banging had given some of the people from the office an excuse to take a break and see what was going on, Random and Luke's father being one of them.

He pulled Luke away from the door first, lifting him down against the wall by the water cooler with its big, translucent blue bottle. Then he swung his arm wide at Random to come over there, as if he were a conductor waving a person to hurry and get on the train. He remembered his father's face being what he called *medium hard*, which was why he hadn't clenched up too tightly inside.

It turned out that he had gauged the situation accurately because all he'd gotten was a routine semitirade at high whisper volume about what would his mother do if she knew he was letting Luke see that kind of carrying on.

Letting him, Random had thought. *Letting* him. Little bastid gets there first when there's anything going on, I don't care where it is. Could be in Okinawa.

But he hadn't said anything out loud.

When their father had finished his minor rebuke, he said,

"Now why don't you two go slide down the chute?" as if that were a novel idea. He went back through the hall to the office, the dark old boards creaking with each step he took.

Random had pulled a Dixie cup from the box on the cracker machine and held it under the spigot on the water bottle until the big air bubble had shot up inside and exploded. When it did, he turned to throw the water on Luke. Evidently Luke had anticipated this move, and all Random saw was the final flappings of the swinging door that led to the loading area at the bottom of the chute.

That had been an unusual Saturday, but today things were normal. Luke was pulling on Random's pants leg, asking for the play-by-play, so Random gave it to him.

Mr. Wendle would stand up at the sink across from him and undo his belt. Then he'd grab each side of the sink, bend half over, and begin to make the first snorting noises in the back of his throat.

When he finished that he would straighten up and lean his head back and commence the actual hawking. Random knew three deep ones was his usual limit, but sometimes the stuff sounded stubborn and he would manage a few more. Random had once witnessed seven, which had to be a record.

Random could imitate all that by bowing and straightening and raring his head back, but the next step was peculiar. Mr. Wendle was a master at it, and to imitate it Random had to let go of the partition with his right hand, losing its support.

At the exact instant between Mr. Wendle's last hawk and his torso's beginning to bend again toward the sink for the unloading, he'd reach the first finger of his right hand down his throat—far enough, it seemed to Random, to measure how much food was left in his stomach from his last meal. Then he'd give it a hefty twist, about a quarter-turn as nearly as Random could estimate.

When he jerked his hand out, his head whipped down almost into the sink as if it were on the end of a string hooked to his finger. The load would come out against the back of the dingy, light-brown bowl.

In a normal hawk Random expected the spitting itself to sound as it was written in comic books, *pitooey,* or something like that. But Mr. Wendle's made no sound at all—there was never any explosion. It seemed as if he just kept his mouth open and the stuff *thropped* out. There wasn't a more accurate word for it.

He could see the result when Mr. Wendle straightened up again and shifted himself sideways to hitch his pants. It was so mean-looking he had to turn his head away the first few times. Lately he hadn't looked at it.

Two or three successful hawkings a visit would usually be sufficient. Random had to go through the pantomime each time, or Luke would get violent with his leg. By the third one Random's left arm would be quivering when he did the finger-in-the-throat part.

What had become more annoying, however, were Luke's recent attempts to find out if he had grown tall enough to see over the partition for himself. Random had compared heights with him in front of the mirror in their bedroom, where it was plain Luke was nowhere near ready. But it had done no good. It was as if Luke thought he'd be taller standing on the sink in the men's room at the warehouse than he was on the floor at home.

Today when Mr. Wendle hitched his pants and decided he needed a third hawk, Luke began to try to climb up again.

He grabbed Random's leg, the same one whose pants he had been in the habit of pulling. Random tried to shake him off, which meant he had to lift the leg and lose half his bracing.

"Jesus, Luke," he hissed, much as his father had hissed at him after the unsuccessful Bridewater rescue attempt, Mr. Wendle started his deep hawking sounds, Luke hit his knee while trying to get it over the edge of the sink and pulled twice as hard on Random's leg for help, Random hissed again, lost his grip on the partition, and what Random was sure anybody a mile away could have seen was going to happen, happened.

He fell off the sink.

It wouldn't be quite accurate to say his mistake was trying not to land on top of his brother. His mistake was *succeeding* in that, because it meant he came down partly on his side and partly on his head against the wall behind him, nearly ending his career, as he might have put it, with his legs sprayed cockeyed across the commode.

He slid slowly down into the space between the wall and the commode and sat there a minute. When he realized there was nothing broken, and focused on Luke standing in the doorway, he let him have it. "Dumb, stupid idiot" and "Goddamned nuisance" were the complimentary beginnings.

He exploded with what were for him the usual words about where Luke could go and what he could eat and some tricks he could perform on himself, but Random noticed even while he was listening to all that coming from his own mouth he could feel it not satisfying him. He felt as if he were warming up for something else.

He heard his voice deepen, as if it belonged to an older person; he told Luke that he was going to go into the other toilet and scrape Mr. Wendle's hawkups off the sink.

"I'm gonna make a wad out of 'em and jam 'em down your throat," he yelled. "Then maybe you won't be so all-fired anxious to get a look at 'em anymore."

When Luke heard that his eyes rounded and bulged out, and he disappeared from the doorway.

Random had no trouble admitting to himself that he had a few usual dreams about torture and revenge on his brother when in the warehouse. They were, he thought, ordinary desires, such as wanting to trap Luke in the middle of four stacks of cement bags and then pour the dust from one of the bags down on his head from the top. Or to pick him up on the prongs of the forklift and drop him down the elevator shaft from the sixth floor.

Sometimes he even wanted to lay him on the railroad tracks

outside of one of the loading doors, but when he went far enough to imagine the way Luke's body would pop open when the freight car rolled over it, he had to stop, so he rejected that one as a serious possibility.

He knew the others weren't serious possibilities either, even though he received serious pleasure from thinking about them. But wanting to choke Luke to death on Mr. Wendle's hawkups was a new one, and he was surprised at its intensity. He came to the point, lying there like stuffing in a turkey, where he thought he might really be able to pull it off.

He wasn't sure how long it was before his hip started to hurt, as if someone were grating metal through it, or exactly when Mr. Wendle poked his moonface around the doorjamb, appeared to stare past him at the wall, and disappeared, but during that time he realized that he was closer to doing what he was thinking than he usually got. He heard again the deepened tone his voice had taken when he had made his promise to Luke, and he felt as if it had been at least six months since Luke had run off.

He dragged himself up and half-limped into the office, rubbing his hip. He figured Luke would most likely be sitting in the chair at the end of their father's desk, chaining paper clips or making chimneys out of the dictaphone cylinders.

But he wasn't there. No one had seen him for half an hour.

His father looked up at Random from the desk. On the top corner of the next sheet in a stack of papers, his thumb was poised. He was just about to whip it up to his face to lick it to help pry the pages apart. Even though Random knew his mouth was twisted oddly getting ready for his thumb, he took his father to be expressing displeasure at his not taking proper care of his little brother.

He took a couple of steps backward and bumped into Mrs. Bull, who was squeezing out of her switchboard cubicle. That helped. "Scuze me," he said gratefully, dodged around her leg, and headed back out to look for Luke.

He made stops at the retail desk, the linoleum room, sporting goods, and the broken-package department, but Luke wasn't in any of them, and nobody had seen him lately, either.

He was just passing the men's rooms again, on his way to the warehouse, when Baker Bridewater seemed to appear out of nowhere. He started talking, saying this and that about nothing, standing between Random and the swinging door. Random thought he was acting strange, and talking too loud, but he wasn't able to figure out why. About the time his curiosity began to show on his face Bridewater stepped around him and went on toward the office. "See you later now," he said, smiling.

"Yeah," Random mumbled and had his arm out to push through the door when he heard a loud thud on the other side of it, some cartons falling over, and Luke's voice letting out a single, Godawful scream.

He rammed through the door and saw Luke lying on his back on the wood floor beyond the end of the chute, what looked like blood all over his neck and cheek, and one of his legs twisted beneath him.

Random had an image of Luke coming around the last turn in the chute out into the straightaway, standing up, as if Random hadn't told him a million times he wasn't ready to try that yet. Random was sure he had come down the last stretch standing up. It had to be.

He ran over to Luke; as he bent down he read *mattock heads* in big blue letters on one of the overturned cartons Luke was lying beside. "Good Lord," he whispered, reaching his hand before he could stop himself and touching the thick red substance on the side of his brother's head.

It was cold and thin.

Cold and thin.

As Random slowly registered that it wasn't warm and sticky and thick, as he knew blood should be, he realized how still everything was. Or how still he was. Or, he wondered, maybe it had been this still all along and he had just walked into it without noticing.

He looked up and saw Mr. Wendle and the packing man watching him, one of the men leaning in the door of the freight car at the loading dock, smiling, even Bridewater standing by the swinging door, holding a ball of twine.

When he heard the laughter he wasn't sure where it had started—perhaps from inside his head, perhaps from all around. He felt for an instant, hearing the sound as if it were its own echo, that those two sources might be the same.

He looked down at his brother.

Luke was grinning. He reached up from what suddenly seemed to Random a long way below, his arms becoming as long as an octopus's tentacles, as if he were going to hug Random down to him.

He didn't.

He wiped ketchup all over Random's face. Random could feel him pushing it onto his cheeks and ears, and what struck him as the funniest part was that his head seemed to nuzzle into Luke's hands and push back, as if it had a will of its own.

Finally Luke took his hands away and Random no longer saw him from a distance; he now seemed shoved up so close that if the space between them diminished any farther he would pass through Random as if he weren't there.

At that moment Luke spat in Random's face, and his and everybody's laughter became very specific—Random could hear each one as if his laughter were a voice, the way each one of them talked—and he saw everything just as it was, not far away or up close but at the exact distance everything was from him, and he got up off his knees and turned and ran into one of the men's rooms, he didn't notice which one, and spent a long time bent over the sink, washing the ketchup off.

SWEET LUCY WINE

I

Sweet Lucy Wine is not a member of Mark Random's family. "She is my legacy from your Aunt Longwood," his mother would say. "It wasn't something I had to do, you understand, but I couldn't live with myself if I didn't take her in."

She would draw down the ends of her mouth and raise her chin so her neck muscles protruded like small ropes being stretched taut. Her eyes would shift off at an angle as if she were looking for somebody else she could tell the underside of the story to, but, as far as Random knew, no one was ever there.

"Anyway," she would say, "nobody asks to be put on this earth, so we have to do what we do."

Sweet Lucy Wine has lived in the Randoms' house for a couple of years, in the front room upstairs, which gives her certain privileges, one of which is eating dinner with the family at the big table in the dining room. So far, however, she hasn't entered the inner circle. When Random's father starts to get up after rubbing his last shred of roll through the last trail of roast-beef gravy, and his wife says, "Aren't you forgetting something?" then Sweet Lucy Wine is not invited to hang around for dessert.

Neither are Random and Luke. If there is dessert.

Random's father hasn't forgotten anything. He won't be able to get his chair in front of the TV as soon as he'd like, which means he'll have to postpone his prime-time nap, probably until he goes to bed. He sighs, or his body goes through the collapsing motion that follows a sigh, and his forty-five-year-old haunches settle back into his seat.

He folds his napkin into a square and sets it beside his mat. His hands then begin a search for an acceptable object to fiddle with. All his utensils are dirty, and Sweet Lucy Wine, or Random, or Luke, depending on whose turn it is this evening, has probably already taken his plate to the kitchen; the napkin ring made from a sea shell has been broken and thrown out, and the centerpiece of cornflowers is just out of reach now that he's put on some extra weight, so his hands float around like leaves on the breeze. He runs them once through his thick, graying hair. By the time his wife begins to tell him what he forgot, they have come to rest, gripping the arms of the chair.

He looks to Random as if he might leap up any second and go tend to something in another room.

Sweet Lucy Wine, Random, and Luke watch TV. Sweet Lucy Wine has a habit of calling herself a "connoisseur of television." She has never watched anything that she hasn't developed a decided opinion on, at least to Random's knowledge. She never hesitates to say what's on her mind, but he pays less attention to what she says than to the way her lipstick gradually disappears from her mouth as she talks.

She watches most of her TV at the Randoms' house, which seems normal to Mark since she lives there, but sometimes she tells him about a program she has seen somewhere else. He doesn't ask where. He has heard his mother say, "Whatever she does outside the house is her business," and he repeats this to himself when the occasion demands it, although not as acerbically.

Once Random happened to notice an open envelope on Sweet Lucy Wine's dresser next to the transparent hairbrush with the letters of a name worn away on it. He had looked inside. It was a love letter. It said, "Sweet Lucy Wine, My Valentine, You make me Shine!" There was a heart colored in purple, and some *X*'s and something else written down near the bottom, but he hadn't read that because his neck had begun to bristle, indicating to him, as he put it, he'd used up his noticing time. As he refolded the letter, he brushed his finger lightly over a blotch at the bottom that looked like the substance he had seen in one of her makeup bottles.

A movie is on, starring Robert Mitchum. Sweet Lucy Wine has seen it, and she begins telling Random and Luke how good it is, all about a preacher who goes from town to town conning widows out of their savings and then deserting them. "He's not a real preacher," she corrects herself. "He has a private arrangement with God which he calls his religion. It lets him do what he wants to do. He's got 'l-o-v-e' tattooed on the fingers of one hand and 'h-a-t-e' on the other. The only sermon he's got is when he hand-wrestles with himself. Love wins."

Sweet Lucy Wine says the problem with movies like that is that the people in them are so dumb. Its opening scene, she says, lets us know how the preacher repeats his routine from town to town, always the same. Find a widow. Make up to her until she marries you. Take her money. Random is impressed, at first, in spite of the preacher's sneer, listening to him describe his recent success. He's riding down a hard-packed county road in an old convertible, talking upwards.

"See," Sweet Lucy Wine says, "this is where the dumbness comes in. All the next widow has to do is watch the movie and she would know not to take up with the preacher, because she would see how bad he is." She looks from the TV set to Random, smiling. "I'd never let Robert Mitchum get near me after learning what he wants. Would you?"

Random, taken off guard, thinks a moment and says, "It would make a short movie."

Her smile fades. She looks at Random as if to say What do you know? as his father comes stomping into the room. He passes close to Random's chair, bumping his leg on it. Random can hear his mother's voice going on in the dining room, as if his father were still sitting at the table. His father steps over Luke sitting in the middle of the floor and Random watches him rummage in the desk drawer over the blotter where he keeps a collection of arcane little books—bank books and budget books and others Random can't identify.

The back of his neck folds up in two or three places, trying to hide the two muscles that run up into his skull, which are as tight as the rawhide ties in Random's moccasins. Random sees Robert Mitchum in prison trying to find out where his cellmate, a murderer about to be executed, has hidden $10,000. His mother's voice continues, its volume increasing—"more than your own children, and you not paying any attention."

His father closes the desk drawer and starts back toward the dining room. Beside Random's chair he stops and looks at the TV a minute. His eyes seem to bulge slightly, reflecting the image on the screen. Random watches him go on into the dining room and sit down. He rests his elbows on the table and starts to leaf through one of the little books.

Sweet Lucy Wine has stopped delivering opinions on the movie. She has crossed one leg over the other and set her head at an angle, so her hair tilts over part of her face. Her eyes don't seem to Random to be looking at anything specific, but he realizes he can't see them too well because she has turned her head away slightly.

Her tilted hair arrests him and he stares at it. He knows her hair tends to get stiff on her. He hears her complaining about that sometimes when he's in her room. She has a jar of some kind of jelly she uses on it when it stiffens. The bluish substance disappears when she rubs it in, but Random likes the way her hair shines for a day or so after she uses it, if the light hits it right. He also likes the fact that her hair is the same deep black color as her eyes.

He turns his attention to the TV again, in time to see Robert Mitchum singing "Leaning on Jesus" while he walks by the next widow's fence in the moonlight. It sounds like a threat, not a hymn. Then a young boy, not too much younger than Random, goes to his bedroom window and watches Mitchum. The boy is the only one who knows where his father has put the $10,000 he killed two people for. Random looks at the blond hair falling across his forehead and his unsuspecting eyes.

Almost before Random knows it, Sweet Lucy Wine has uncrossed her legs, stood up, smoothed her skirt in front and behind, and gone out the front door. Probably doesn't have any more opinions on the movie, Random thinks.

He's involved with it, though, and is settling into his chair after Sweet Lucy Wine leaves, when his mother enters. "You sitting here watching the TV and your brother's up in the trees again. What are you good for anyhow? Get out there and get him down from those trees this instant, before I get the switch."

He's taller than she is, and heavier, but he moves. He doesn't even turn off the TV, which sometimes has been a switching offense itself. But this time he knows it won't matter. Priorities are priorities, even though his "little" brother has long since learned to climb trees and needs no real looking after. As he passes the door to the dining room he sees that his father has rolled up his sleeves and hung his tie on the arm of his chair.

He goes outside and walks across the yard, which is made of dust because he and his friends have kept the grass from growing on it over the years by playing marbles and mumbledepeg all the time. His mother wants grass. "The neighbors have grass," she frequently says. His father always answers, "Why plant seed when all they're going to do is rub the grass off as soon as it starts to grow?" When he says that, Sweet Lucy Wine nods her head.

Luke is sitting in the mimosa. Thank goodness he's not in one of the oaks, Random thinks, or the maple with the split planks on the side. He's impossible to get down from the oaks. But the mimosa is small, and is dying from having been climbed so often. Some of the branches have been cut off, too. Random knows he can get up there and pull Luke out with relatively little trouble.

While he's walking to the mimosa he wonders if Sweet Lucy Wine is behind Luke's being in it. He's been staying out of the trees lately, for a month anyway, since school let out for the summer. Their mother hates his climbing the trees because she says it's going to be the death of her, his getting in places he can get hurt while she's busy with something else that has to be done.

"Can't watch you two all the time and keep the house straight, and manage your father, too," she says, her mouth scrunching up. "Why don't you look out after your brother like you're supposed to, and help take the load off me? Makes me tired." Random believes her. She seems tired most of the time. He hears her tell his father she is. His father doesn't cuss very often, especially when Sweet Lucy Wine is within earshot, but when the subject of being tired is introduced into a conversation Random has noticed he tends to let up. He's heard him say things like *Oh, shit, woman, not again,* and *Damnitalltohell,* running it together so that Random sees one word in his mind, as if it were a television screen.

What causes him to wonder about Sweet Lucy Wine and his brother is that he sees her sitting in the swing under the willow when he leaves the house. She's swaying back and forth a little, biting her fingernail, her hair leaning the same way he had seen it in front of the TV. Her sandals hang off her toes, dragging in the dust. He notices most of the paint has chipped off her toenails.

"Come on down out of there," he calls to his brother.

Luke is sitting on one of the upper branches and sticks his tongue out at him. "Smart," he says. "Smart. Come on down now. I don't want to miss too much of the movie."

Random is sure the young boy will outlast Mitchum, but he wants to know how. He particularly wants to see the boy on his own, with his sister on the river, which Sweet Lucy Wine has mentioned to him.

Sweet Lucy Wine calls from the swing, "Stay up there all night, Luke. Use your feet."

"Big help you are," Random calls back, getting his heels set in the two crotches just below his brother. He reaches up and gets a grip on Luke's waist, fixing to haul him down into his arms.

Luke hangs onto the branches for a second or two, then lets go, as he always does, and clamps his fingers like a bat's into Random's hair, and pulls it. Although he's slight for his age, Random has to struggle with him, keeping his balance from practice and familiarity with the mimosa. Sweet Lucy Wine is yelling something from the swing, but all Random can hear is the noise. He thinks, I'm doing the best I can.

He scrapes his elbow on the trunk as he finally lets go and Luke jumps down. Luke spits at him but he's too high up and the spit arcs in the air and falls on the ground. By the time it hits, Luke is already interested in something else.

Random climbs down and starts back to the house. Luke walks over to Sweet Lucy Wine and whispers something into her ear. She giggles, and shifts so he can ease up into her lap in the swing. He's almost too big for this, but they manage. She lets her sandals fall into the dust when they start swinging.

Random slams the door. As he goes into the room where the TV is he sees his father still sitting at the dining room table, leaning on his elbows, the little books scattered around in front of him. His eyes are closed, and he's releasing his breath from his lips in a long, deep blow. Random can hear his mother in the kitchen. She turns the water off, and as he sits down in time for the final two parts of the movie, he hears a dish bump against the sink.

2

How long, Random asks himself, can Sweet Lucy Wine sit out there swinging with Luke in her lap? She's singing "I Never Get Enough of That Wonderful Stuff." Which I hate. Luke just gazes off into the oak leaves on the upswing, and into the dust on the down.

Luke, he thinks. My crapass little brother. Sitting there. He'll probably grow up spending half his life at the dinner table star-

ing at his lettuce or spinach or turnip greens hours after everybody else has finished and gone about their business, and the
other half in somebody's lap.

But something could happen.

Random could be sitting on the porch after a movie, and his
cousin Lord Jack Hart could drive up. Doing the unexpected was
Lord Jack's habit. His most famous trick occurred at the beach
when he drove a TV star's rented Coupe de Ville down the side of
one of the stone jetties that jut out every mile or so into the
ocean. Random thought the piled-up stones resembled lizard
tails. He had thought getting a car onto one would be impossible, but Lord Jack did it. And not just on the jetty but way out,
almost to the point where the tail became thinner than the car.

Lord Jack was talking to Random and Wonderbuns, Lord
Jack's girl. She was in the back seat. Lord Jack was pretending to
be a TV star. He was saying things like "I tire of Waikiki," in the
tone of an aristocrat afflicted with ennui.

Wonderbuns would laugh and lean toward the front seat so
Random could smell her hair, or something, and pretend to hold
a cigarette holder like Bette Davis and say, "But Lord Jack, how
can you *think* of leaving such a *mahvlus* place?" and blow fake
smoke toward the windshield.

The car would bump and lurch on the jetty, its side scraping
rocks, the smaller ones kicking out from under the wheels and
whanging against the bottom. Lord Jack would tell Wonderbuns
how he *knew*, but he had had so many *offers*, "and besides, it's
been *done*."

Whenever Lord Jack would say that, he and Wonderbuns
would look at each other and go blank, and then break into
spasms of laughter.

They stopped, however, when the car began to tip toward the
water. Lord Jack pulled his foot off the accelerator and yelled,
"Lean to the left." The car seemed to Random to be making up
its mind whether to topple into the ocean or not. Wonderbuns

moved all the way over behind Lord Jack, and Random squeezed up tightly next to him. Finally they felt the Cadillac settle enough for them to get out.

Random was hearing himself sigh and say "Whew," and wondering how they had gotten this far out anyhow, realizing that he hadn't noticed how much distance they'd come while Lord Jack and Wonderbuns had been carrying on, when he was astonished to see that the two of them had commenced to cheer. They seemed suddenly no more than a pom-pom girl and a drum major at a football game.

> Lean to the left,
> Lean to the right,
> Stand up, sit down,
> Fight, fight, fight.

They enacted the cheer, too, while they called it. After Wonderbuns faked socking Lord Jack in the jaw they stared at each other, Wonderbuns' right arm hooked out into her fist and Lord Jack's head thrown back as if she'd really hit him, getting that blank expression Random saw so often he could swear they practiced it. Then, laughing, they collapsed against each other on the rocks.

Wonderbuns got her name because of her striking figure overall, not just one part of it. When Random and his friends spoke of her, they stressed proportion rather than size. She was neither stretched out of shape nor the object of snide remarks or references to corrective surgery. In fact, Random had never heard anyone refer in a disparaging manner to Wonderbuns' particular endowment. She was good-natured about it, too. She would meet new boys and sing, "Look away, look away, Dixieland," smiling her broad smile, looking at them with her generous brown eyes.

Everyone agreed she and Lord Jack were a pair.

They could drive up in the Ford Lord Jack had bought, used, a month ago for his graduation.

Random thought Lord Jack's arrival would throw Sweet Lucy Wine. She would stop swinging by dragging her feet through the dust, making a faint gouge where her toes raked it. She would be sitting there holding Luke, the color fading slightly from her face, and her expression fading, too, as if something inside her were raising its hand to be excused.

Luke looks up at her. "Lucy," he says—it's almost a question—and reaches his hand up onto her shoulder.

She's staring off at nothing, in the direction of Lord Jack's car, which he has stepped out of. She seems to Random to be looking at the place where he just was. Since he's moving, the place where he was is moving, too, so even if Sweet Lucy Wine is looking at empty space her eyes follow it across the yard.

Luke asks her name again and pushes her shoulder. She looks down at his hand. She pats it and then picks it off by the fingers as if it were an object she intended to return to its owner. Luke lets her put it in his lap.

"You go on now," she says in an even tone, quietly. She is staring past Luke at the dust where her scuff marks are. She brushes some hair from her forehead with the back of her wrist so her head turns a little, but her eyes remain aimed at the ground.

It's as if Luke has answered a question instead of asked one, and she is telling him, as a teacher who is old and tired might, *Yes, that's right. You can go back to your life now.*

Other people, Random thinks. Other people.

He has stood up on the porch. He smiles at Lord Jack coming across the yard, and looks him in the eye, but his attention is on Wonderbuns walking on his right. She's wearing short jeans with ragged edges, torn off at the upper thighs, and a boy's tank top with thousands of air holes in it; Random has trouble not looking at it, doubling the usual problem he has when he sees somebody built like Wonderbuns. He's aware of trying not to look at the open armpit, the tightness of the top, the little holes that let him see the peach color of her bra, all at the same time.

"You doing anything?" Lord Jack sits down on the stoop

where Random had been and looks out at Sweet Lucy Wine. She's gotten out of the swing and is standing still looking at Luke run around the side of the house. She looks as if she is making up her mind about something.

Random sits down again a step behind Lord Jack and to his left. Sweet Lucy Wine seems almost a different person to him when Lord Jack is there. Thinner, darker, as if she recedes into herself. He feels as if he'd have a harder time talking to her.

But he also thinks it might not be Lord Jack at all. He looks up at Wonderbuns' auburn hair, loose on her shoulders, and the pale skin that he can still see even under her new tan.

"Whatever I'm doing," he says. "You?"

"Ridin' around. Want to go to the drive-in?"

Wonderbuns sticks out her tennis shoe and pushes Lord Jack's knee so it swings once, and comes back. She does it again, resting the shoe on Lord Jack's knee, a grin on her face trying not to be a grin. When Lord Jack looks at her, Random sees her turn her eyes off toward the oak trees, about halfway up. She seems to him to be pretending she did something sneaky and is trying to hide how proud she is of it.

Lord Jack pushes her foot off his knee, and Random can tell he's looking hard at Wonderbuns because his jaw tightens and a little muscle in his neck pops out in a ridge.

Smells change about that time, Random feels the air suddenly develop a thin edge on it, and Sweet Lucy Wine says, "Excuse me." She crosses between Lord Jack and Wonderbuns, letting the forefinger of her left hand rest on Lord Jack's shoulder just for a second for balance. Random sees that as clearly as if it were on a stage in slow motion, or in a photograph. But he doesn't see her pass him by.

She goes into the house, letting the screen door bang. Random listens to her sandals flop up the stairs inside.

"Yeah," he says. "Sure." Then for some reason he says, "No. Not really." He stands up and puts his hands in the pockets of his khakis. He inserts the toe of his right tennis shoe between the cast-iron railings of the stoop, and twists it slowly. His foot inside the shoe turns, but the toe of his shoe doesn't. He stares at the distortion caused by the pressure.

When he looks up, Lord Jack and Wonderbuns are going off in Lord Jack's Ford, around the corner.

He takes his toe out and kicks the railing once, hard. He doesn't feel a thing.

———

It's easier to say what Random and his friends didn't envy Lord Jack for than what they did. It wasn't that he could do a lot of things better than any of the rest of them, which no one disputed. When they played touch football on the median in the street in front of Rafer McBride's house, Lord Jack would be the primary receiver and catch everything. Three or four people would try to cover him, and the passer would pledge not to run so the defense wouldn't have to rush anybody. At least one person would usually get his hands on the ball, but Lord Jack would catch it anyway, the others having been faked out. Some would inevitably wind up lying in the grass. Random thought it was like trying to get the ball out of the bird claws on the end of a table leg.

It wasn't that he was bigger or older, either, both of which were true. The aunts and uncles used to remark how neat he kept himself. One had to agree with them. His collar was always white and lay evenly on his shoulders no matter what he'd been doing. What impressed Random was that somehow Lord Jack could make being neat seem like not such a big deal.

No one could remember his ever falling down.

It wasn't Wonderbuns, either, although everyone secretly wished he could be so lucky. It was general knowledge they'd get married one day. How soon depended on whether or not Lord Jack took the football scholarship to the state university. He was taking his time making up his mind. When Random started high school next fall, Lord Jack would already be a legend.

It seemed to Random that beneath everything else Lord Jack had the future under his thumb. He admitted he couldn't explain exactly what he meant by that. It wasn't that Random thought Lord Jack would live forever, or never get old and dribble from the side of his mouth like their uncle Seldom did, or not make mistakes. It was more that he was on top of all the possibilities. Whatever might come, Lord Jack made it seem as if he would have a say in its coming, as if nothing were going to touch him he couldn't fit into his life. Tomorrow might have its secrets and surprises, Lord Jack's life seemed to say, but when it gets here it can't be much different from today. And he handled today just fine. Some people said Lord Jack was too simple, but to Random simple or complicated didn't apply. To him Lord Jack was the only person he'd ever met who was all in one piece, like a sky with no clouds in it.

And everybody seemed to like him. Even Rafer McBride admitted liking him to a degree, and that was saying a lot because even though Rafer didn't make it a business to *dis*like people, he could have. Sometimes if he couldn't find an obvious reason not to like somebody, he'd present something based on information no one else had heard of.

Rafer had a saying he trotted out frequently to express his general outlook on life. He'd made a jingle of it, which he performed with a weird, thin smile that made him look to Random like an animal ready to tear the hide off a new carcass. He sang it so often the others thought of it as his motto:

> Damnation,
> Motherfuck,
> If you've been born
> You're out of luck.

The jingle always led Random to the other aspect of Rafer's attitude toward Lord Jack: he admitted Lord Jack was all right, but he had a reservation about it. Everyone figured he had to;

that was his way: Random knew if you pushed Rafer into a corner and made him admit something, you could count on his having a reservation ready to balance things.

With Lord Jack he said that anybody who had as good luck as Lord Jack early in life would just as well die at about twenty, because you could be sure something would crash down on his head to make up for it.

He didn't find any contradiction between that and his motto, either. He said with Lord Jack all it amounted to was that being out of luck got postponed. Which to his mind was worse because if you weren't careful, you began thinking life was pretty good, which made the truth that much harder to deal with when it came. Rafer had told Random several times that he didn't think Lord Jack was careful enough, by a long shot.

One weekend Rafer composed a song about Lord Jack. He sang it to Random—a sort of fast-paced country beat with a fake twang in his voice—accompanying himself on the guitar:

DO I WANT TO BE LORD JACK?

His bird ain't in the book,
Can't type, can't cook
But goes down on her back—
Do I wanna be Lord Jack?

Got away with good luck and never should.
Nobody's life should be that good.
I don't want to be Lord Jack.

It ain't possible to be that stacked.
If they're real
I'd like a feel—
Do I wanna be Lord Jack?

When you're too good to be true
Life will catch up with you.
I don't want to be Lord Jack.

Nobody pretends to know who's right, of course, Rafer or Lord Jack, or somebody else who thinks differently. Random once ventured the opinion that whether it's under Lord Jack's thumb or not, the future is going to be what it is.

"What I really care about," Random mutters now, standing on the porch, "is it could happen that way. Lord Jack could drive up. That would get Sweet Lucy Wine off the swing, and Luke out of her lap, for a while at least. It probably wouldn't change Lord Jack's life any, or get the Coupe de Ville off the jetty. But I would have to remember the way Sweet Lucy Wine balanced herself on Jack's shoulder with nothing but the tip of her finger, and me not even seeing her go by."

3

"I couldn't take that," he says.

He knows he couldn't, even without having to imagine Sweet Lucy Wine upstairs in her room with the curtains billowing in full of air, and not knowing whose trouble it was she was up there, hers or his own.

He was sure his foot would start to hurt, too. Not a mark on his shoe from the railing—it was painted a glossy, rustproof black—but his toes would probably swell. He thought that tending to them would be one more straw on his mother's camel, or however that saying of hers went.

Another thing he had to consider was, with Sweet Lucy Wine upstairs and Lord Jack gone, he could stay outside in the dust with his brother, or go inside and watch his mother and father go through their ritual of looking at something besides each other until bedtime.

His father might have gone to sleep in his chair by now. Put the little books away. Sometimes he could sleep no matter what.

But he knew all his mother would have done was to come down a notch in her fume.

He decided that even if he could have taken it, Sweet Lucy Wine going by the way she did, the rest of the world made him feel like there had to be a better way.

But with that thought came a hesitation, as if he could hear Rafer McBride say in his head, "Don't count on it."

Lord Jack didn't spend any time on the porch, he thought. Forget all that. He just drove up, honked his horn, got out for a minute with Wonderbuns, didn't even turn off the engine, waved across the yard at me as if Sweet Lucy Wine weren't even there. Then they were gone. By now he and Wonderbuns are parked out at Boyster's Dam, picking dewberries.

But he does allow himself to come out and sit down on the porch steps after the movie.

He looks out at the dust and plays one of his favorite fantasies, wanting the front yard to be a wide, open prairie, with wheat swaying on it and train tracks running off into the distance. He imagines it a shimmering gray-green with flecks of silver scattered in it.

But it's the front yard.

"What else is new?" he yells to Sweet Lucy Wine.

She's been in the swing all this time, he has no problem with that, but Luke is bound to have been in and out of it, running around and playing in the dust. "Dumb, chickenshit brother," he mumbles, watching Luke climb up into her lap again.

Sweet Lucy Wine looks up at him over Luke's head. They are barely going back and forth. It's as if a little breeze is moving them, only there isn't one.

"You are," she says. She lifts her right hand off Luke's shoulder and curls it around the swing rope on that side. "Mitchum get his?"

"Sure he did," Random says. "You ever know the bad guy not to? Does your heart good how he gets it every time." He bows his back over and stretches it and mumbles to himself again, "Wish it happened that way in real life."

He looks out from under his eyebrows at the swing. Luke's face and her face appear to him as if they're on the same body, one coming out as he'd expect it to and the other, Luke's, coming out cranksided and no-necked. He can't figure out how such a creature can turn and look up at itself, but it does.

He stands up on the middle step and says loud enough for them to hear him, "Don't know why I watch anything."

"Helps you hide from yourself," Sweet Lucy Wine says.

"Well, aren't you on top of everything?" he says. "Looks like you aren't so bad at hiding, either."

She takes her right hand off the swing rope and puts it around Luke's waist. She gives a little push with her bare feet and they swing back farther. She sticks her toes out when they come toward Random.

"Give your sandals away for your birthday?" he asks her. For some reason, even though his brother is in the way and it doesn't really happen, he sees her legs naked all the way up to her crotch, held together like a diver's but pointed at him instead of disappearing into the water.

So he walks down the steps and onto the sidewalk and tries to take a look. In fact, Sweet Lucy Wine's skirt is bunched up so Luke can get his butt onto the swing seat, but some of it still drapes over her legs. He sees her sandals, too, leaning up against the trunk of the willow.

He has an impulse to walk to the swing and lift Luke out of it and dump him off the Empire State Building like Captain Marvel making the world safe for heroes, but before he can act on it Sweet Lucy Wine takes her arm away and gives Luke a shove from behind.

He doesn't seem to mind, but pops off the swing and wanders toward the porch.

Sweet Lucy Wine doesn't alter her skirt. She sits in the swing with her elbows holding the ropes and her hands hanging toward her lap. She looks up at Random.

"What do you call that girl?" she says.

"Wonderbuns," he says. As far as he knows there's nobody else she could be talking about.

She laughs. It's her regular laugh, coming up out of her stomach and chest. If the air could be cleaned, Random thinks, and a laugh do the cleaning, it would be her laugh.

He smiles. He can't help it. "One of a kind," he says.

"You've got your numbers mixed up," she says, finishing her laugh. She lowers her hands into her lap. "But she's got it down better than most girls her age, I'll give her that."

"What down?"

Sweet Lucy Wine has been looking at Random, but when he asks that question her eyes seem to click as if they hadn't been focused before. He realizes he doesn't have anything to do with his hands, so he puts them in his pockets.

"The routine," she says. He draws a line in the dust with his left sneaker. "Don't worry about it," she says, "your time'll come."

He draws another line in the first one. He feels himself thinking *I don't like to be left out of things,* but he doesn't feel anything, which puzzles him.

"So what?" he says. "We can't all be little blond boys saved by some old lady in the sky."

"Nobody loses all the time, either," she says, and gets out of the swing. She looks at him with that click in her eyes again, both of them standing not eight feet apart. "If you weren't so sweet you'd be tiresome," she says. It doesn't sound as if she intends anything mean by that.

She smiles at him and turns toward the house. Her maroon skirt whirls a little at the edges. He knows her black hair can disappear into the dark when it gets dark, which it will soon. He doesn't mind not being able to stop any of that, but he does say, "Sweet?" to her back as if he has acid in his mouth.

His mother comes out the front door. She wipes her hands on her apron, holding it out in front of her as if she's trying to give it to somebody. Random thinks she may be in the early stages of another swivet, but it's hard to tell.

"Where's your brother?" she asks him.

Sweet Lucy Wine hasn't looked back at him since he spoke, and things seem to him to be getting more and more unfinished. She climbs the steps and pulls the screen door open to go in. She has to squeeze by sideways because his mother is standing in her way. He sees her light-brown hand let the door shut quietly and then draw away inside and disappear. All that's left for him to look at is screen wire, the evening light dying in it. And his mother, the real one he can't do anything about, staring at him across the dust.

Before she can ask him again he says, "I don't know. How am I supposed to know? He's not my child. I don't have anything to do with what the little sumbitch does. He can take care of himself. How come every time I get a little air to move around in somebody's got to—"

He stops. It's not so much that he's surprised at what he's saying—which he is, a little—but at who he sounds like.

Her, he thinks. *I sound like her.*

He realizes that he has an opportunity to be practicing a preamble to a Declaration of Independence, and instead he's complaining and carrying on just like his mother.

"Shit," he says softly, turning away. "Goddamn keep your little brother safe for the world gospel pie never changes, it just gets sliced up different ways."

Rafer McBride's voice in my head was right, he thinks. It looks to him as if no matter how he does it everybody winds up separate. Only the opposite seems true, too. Sweet Lucy Wine's gone again, leaving him with a picture of her hand, and Luke is not only out of the swing but out of his sight as well. But his old lady's wringing her hands at him in her apron, simply by her presence and carriage of body charging him with crimes he doesn't even know exist, and he's standing in the front-yard marble circle listening to some of her voice come out of his mouth.

"It doesn't do any good to talk," he mutters. "I may be learning that much." But not altogether, it seems, because he looks up to Sweet Lucy Wine's open window, not caring if she's watching or listening, or even there, and yells, "Sweet? Shit. I'll show you sweet."

He looks back at his mother, her eyes like a wall with the mortar falling out, and turns and walks away around the side of the house, thinking, *If she believes I'm going after Luke she may be right, but not the way she thinks.*

MR. MANN

Mark Random's grandmother made Sweet Lucy Wine sleep in the basement. Saying it that way expressed what it felt like to him, but the actual truth—"head truth," he called it—was that she lived in the basement room that had been built, years ago, for a maid. Sweet Lucy Wine had, in fact, become a maid for his grandmother, or a helper, at least part of the time, since Mark's mother had made her move out of their house.

"Sure," his grandmother said when his mother asked her if Sweet Lucy Wine could have the maid's old room.

"I can't just throw her out in the street," his mother said, her arms folded in front of her thin chest. "Lord knows it's what I ought to do, but the poor child . . ."

Her voice sounded to Random as if it pranced up to his grandmother's face and stopped. His grandmother didn't seem to know exactly what his mother was carrying on about, and her expression didn't register on his mother, who so far hadn't been looking at anyone while she talked. Random was familiar with this habit of his mother's. She would stare at an object off behind the person as if she were rendering judgment on it. She stared hard, too, Random thought, as if at any moment she would pass sentence, and execute it.

He had seen, too, on other people's faces, his grandmother's look of wondering *What's going on?* when his mother was talking to them. On the other hand, his mother wasn't the only person he'd heard say *poor child* when she meant the opposite. And Sweet Lucy Wine was no child, either.

"It's not altogether her fault, anyway," his mother said to the front hall rug, her voice modulating into a lower-volume seethe. She dropped her arms to her sides, pressing her fists into her thighs. She looked to Random as if she wanted to stomp her foot through the floor, like Rumpelstiltskin.

"When will she be coming?" his grandmother asked, swiping at a wisp of gray hair that had straggled down her forehead.

His mother looked up from the rug at his grandmother as if she finally had found an acceptable verdict, instead of just the agreeable old lady Random loved, who could also fry a mean chicken.

"Oh," she said. "Well, this afternoon."

"All right," his grandmother said, spreading her fingers out and wiping her left palm down her apron. "I'll fix up the maid's room."

Random thought it wasn't such a bad room. It was furnished with a double bed that had brass knobs on the corners, a thing Sweet Lucy Wine called a "vanity" painted orange-brown, and a straight rocker in the corner. A light bulb protruded from an upside-down funnel in the ceiling. Its on-off string hung down to Random's nose.

Sweet Lucy Wine kept her clothes hanging in a big wardrobe with the veneer on the double doors warped, and peeling at the edges. Random liked to shut his eyes and run his fingers over the rippled surface, which felt like those roofs made of split terracotta pipes looked to him, only a lot smaller. He would do that when he sat on the edge of the bed and one of the doors of the wardrobe was partly open.

What made the room special was its being raised on a platform six inches above the floor, so if water backed up in the basement the furniture wouldn't be damaged. The drain was on the other side of the basement, in front of the door to the closet where a toilet and sink and bathtub had been installed.

"I miss the TV," Sweet Lucy Wine says.

Random rubs his fingers over the wavy wood on the door. He gives it a push with his thumb and it floats up against some clothes inside and comes back toward him in slow motion, as if there were syrup on the hinges.

"But I don't have to put up with no more inspections," she says, jerking her brush up and down through a snag in her hair. "That's something anyway."

Her eyes look in the mirror at Random, and he looks down at the bedcovers smunched up against the wood poles at the foot. He pushes the door again and rolls over backwards and out of the bed on the other side.

"You goin'?" she asks.

"I guess." He backs out of the room, holding the doorframe with both hands for balance, stepping down onto the cool cement.

She turns around with her arm still up to her hair. He sees the sweat making a U on her dress in her armpit, and the muscle running over it into her bosom. It seems larger stretched like that. She says, "I'll be up by the time Mr. Mann gets here," and smiles, not so much at Random as at whatever she's thinking about.

She turns half toward him and begins to pick hairs from the brush. "He comes today," she says, "don't he?"

"I guess," he says.

He does. They both know he does. Every Friday, regularly, to bring Random's grandmother chickens for Sunday dinner and the next week. She's one of the few people who still buy from him, preferring the freshly killed birds to the packaged ones in the supermarket, and liking the old ways, too.

Before Random can spin out upstairs Sweet Lucy Wine says, "Do me a favor. Leave the latch off the outside door when you go out."

It doesn't matter to him which door he uses, so he says, "Sure," and leaves her smiling in the mirror at where he was.

The next time he sees her, in about an hour, she looks to him as if she's going to get her picture taken.

He's in the backyard standing next to Mr. Mann's chicken crates, which look like cages to him because of the wooden bars on their sides. They remind him of the foot and head of Sweet Lucy Wine's bed, only those poles are smooth, finished walnut, while the crates are a faded gray, and dried out. He couldn't run his fingers up and down around them without getting a load of splinters.

Two dead chickens are lying still on the grass beside him, some blood speckled on the white feathers below their necks. Another one is flapping and lurching all over the place, headless, with some of its feathers sticking out like quills on a porcupine. If he hadn't known better, he'd have thought they were trying to fly between the time Mr. Mann wrung their heads off and their final twitches. Of course, it was only reflexive nervous spasms; Rafer McBride had told him that a hanged man bounces on the rope for the same reason, and wets his pants.

He watches Mr. Mann get ready to twist the head off another chicken. He didn't swing them around his head like a lasso, as Random had heard some people do. He held the neck with one hand and the head with the other and twisted—it looked like one motion, though, so it didn't exactly seem that he held them at all. Random heard him talk to them, too, low and softly, almost crooning, before he actually did anything.

Mr. Mann once said it was more likely he was talking to himself, but it reminded Random of the way his mother sounded playing with his little brother when he was a baby. She would bend over him, swaddled in diapers in his crib, and prod his ruddy belly with her finger or jiggle his pink foot, cooing at him. The rhythmical lilt, rising and falling, was almost hypnotic. Random once caught himself wanting to take his brother's place, or tear his leg off, or both.

Whatever way Random talked about it, his perception of the act itself never seemed to focus sharply enough. One second there would be a white chicken under Mr. Mann's big-knuckled hands and the next second its head would be on the grass, Mr. Mann standing there, and the rest of the chicken trying to take off. Occasionally Random felt his own forearms quivering slightly, as if he had done the killing, or had wanted to.

Random looks past Mr. Mann an instant before he twists off number four and sees Sweet Lucy Wine on the top step of the back porch. Her hair is shining in the sun, like a million tiny bubbles in a coal pile. She has put on deep red lipstick and a halter dress Random hasn't seen before. It rimples across her bosom, peach-colored, and cuts down from her armpits. He imagines it must be awfully low in back.

He hears Mr. Mann talking gently to the chicken, and his own throat seems to vibrate a little, as if he were humming to himself. Then he sees the blur of Mr. Mann going through his singular motion, and the divided chicken plunges off into the huge for-sythia bush Random and his friends used to use for hide-and-seek. Random notices Mr. Mann is still holding onto the head, and looking at Sweet Lucy Wine.

Random hears the *snip, snip* as she comes down the steps, her legs sideways in high heels in the narrow spaces, the little rivulets between muscles in her calves deepening and becoming shallow with each step.

A hot melting slides from his chest through his groin and legs, and his throat becomes small enough to choke a beebee. He knows right then he would do anything Sweet Lucy Wine asked him to do, if she ever asked him to do anything.

She steps down onto the flagstones and smiles. "Afternoon," she says, looking at Mr. Mann.

"Afternoon," he says. He lets go the chicken head. It drops on the grass.

She walks past the house out to the street and begins to look at the crates left on Mr. Mann's pickup. Random notices her dress isn't only low in back, as he expected, it hangs on her like it wants to be her skin. *Pretty* isn't enough word for it.

Mr. Mann has finished with the last chicken and is piling the crates on the truck and talking to Sweet Lucy Wine almost before Random realizes it. Random dodges number five on his way to the house and some blood spatters on his pants. He sits on the porch steps and rubs the spots with his hand until the cloth is warm. He can hear Sweet Lucy Wine and Mr. Mann laughing.

Sometimes when Sweet Lucy Wine was still living in the Randoms' house she would sit on the front stoop and play her guitar. Random remembered spring evenings when everything was slowing down for summer but was still tense, too, as if a volcano were heating up to blow its top.

Rafer McBride would come by sometimes and listen. Once Random remembered Rafer reaching down over Sweet Lucy Wine and strumming her guitar with his right hand. He told her, "C, C, F, and C," and she fretted those chords while he sang:

> Music in the soul
> Music in the soul
> Almost as good
> As a peter in the hole.

He could see Rafer's head set in beside Sweet Lucy Wine's, as if they were people in a painting, both of them looking down at his fingers while he played. She smiled when he finished and sang "Rock of Ages," and she and Rafer nearly broke up laughing.

Random thinks the laughter he hears now is like that, only deeper.

"Is he done?" His grandmother's voice comes through the screen door behind him.

"Yes'm. I reckon. He's putting the crates on the truck."

She comes out, hitches up her dress, and Random edges over so she can get by. As she passes him she lets her hand rest lightly on his head. At the bottom of the steps she lets go of her skirt and apron, and looks up at him.

"Are you planning to help me pluck today?"

"I don't know," Random says. "Maybe."

"Busy schedule, hunh?" she says, smiling. "You all right? You look kind of mopey."

"Yes'm. I'm fine. Just don't seem to be able to get started, I guess."

She goes into the yard to collect the dead chickens, and he knows that today he's not going to be able to watch. As he stands up, the forsythia seems to swell from the inside like the top of a giant mushroom rising from the ground.

He goes through the porch and into the kitchen. The scalding pot is already on the stove heating. It looks to him big enough to hold all five chickens at once, even though he knows it isn't, and the heat in the kitchen makes his skin prickle. He puts his arms around himself, as if to keep his chest from turning inside out, and runs through the back hall and down the basement steps.

The sudden coolness feels good to him. He stops at the bottom and breathes deeply, feeling it run from his feet up through his body and into his head. Then he walks into Sweet Lucy Wine's room and curls up on her bed.

He doesn't notice how long he lies there, his head tucked into a fold in the bunched-up covers so he can smell his breath mixed up with what he supposes are Sweet Lucy Wine's body smells. It's warm and he relaxes, remembering the doctors putting the mask on him before they took his tonsils out, asking him to count backwards from one hundred. He had made it to ninety-six.

He doesn't count this time, but he dozes deeply enough that the sound of the outside door opening wakes him suddenly, as a gunshot might.

At first he figures it's Sweet Lucy Wine, but he doesn't understand why she would try to be so quiet about everything. He recognizes it as one of those times you can *hear* the person trying *not* to make noise, he's trying so hard. Random starts to sweat; he's curious to find out who it is, but he doesn't want to be discovered himself, so he eases off the bed and crawls into one side of the wardrobe, settling down on a pile of Sweet Lucy Wine's dirty clothes.

He pulls the door almost closed. Through the crack he sees Mr. Mann stick his beady little head in the door, look around as if he were in a movie, and then step up into the room.

By the time he hears Sweet Lucy Wine at the top of the basement stairs taking that polite tone with his grandmother he had heard her use when she was trying to cut short conversation with his mother, Mr. Mann has taken his shirt and trousers off, and is trying to unhang his big toe from the top of his shorts. Random notices he's wearing the boxer kind.

Like my father, he thinks. Not hugnuts, like me. His pecker's half up, too. Looks like a cooked chicken neck, only redder.

Mr. Mann's face is flushed, and Random thinks his eyes are swimming in a part of the river he's been in before, and likes.

When Sweet Lucy Wine comes in Random watches her look Mr. Mann up and down in the middle. He can tell Mr. Mann wants to glue himself to her and run away from her at the same time. Mr. Mann waves his arms at her to shut the door, which she does without taking her eyes off of him.

Except for one thing, the rest is a blur in Random's memory, until they sneaked out of the room and Sweet Lucy Wine let Mr. Mann out of the basement. Random has no idea how long it lasted, and as far as he's concerned it could have been everywhere. Even if he were put in a room with Sweet Lucy Wine, or somebody else, he knew he couldn't remember enough of what they did to repeat it. *I know what goes where,* he thought, *but this was different.*

He remembered it as though the two people were a thrashing, rolling animal, full of itself, abnormally swollen, with extra arms and legs. He saw a smear of Sweet Lucy Wine's lipstick across some part of Mr. Mann's pasty skin. He wanted to close the door of the wardrobe when things got so mixed up he couldn't tell who was who, but he also wanted to jump on Mr. Mann's back with the hair running down beside the middle, as he saw it, and to beat on him, drive him into Sweet Lucy Wine so far he couldn't get out, or tear him out of there and take his place himself, if he could be sure he wouldn't get cooked. He experienced the melting sensation again, and wanted to rub one of the glistening poles on the headboard.

He may have wanted to choke the shit out of everybody, for all he knew. But he couldn't remember much of anything besides the confusion, theirs and his own.

Except for the one thing: how Sweet Lucy Wine undressed. She would have lost a race with butter melting on a stack of lukewarm pancakes. Her body glowed like polished furniture, too, and looked as if it created a thin slick of moisture on itself. She became the word *glide* in his head.

Afterwards they sneaked out of the room, and when Random heard them mumbling and snuggling outside the door he decided he'd better move.

His plan was to slip across the basement while they were around the corner saying good-bye, hide in the bathroom in the tub behind the shower curtain until Sweet Lucy Wine went back to her room, and then head upstairs and out of there.

He managed the first part successfully, but the trouble was, after Sweet Lucy Wine snapped the latch on the outside door she inserted herself into part two of his plan.

The bathroom.

Mighta known, he thought. After all the other stuff I've gone through today, now I've got to be cool. He figured he had to endure maybe five more minutes. God forbid she was gonna take a shower. No, he told himself, she's just coming in here to do some woman business, and that'll be that.

When the light switched on and he heard Sweet Lucy Wine adjusting herself on the commode, he froze. Standing there, he thought of how good the grass in the backyard was going to feel between his toes. He stared at the pink flowers on the shower curtain, which looked darker with the light on behind them, and he resisted an urge to rub his hands on his thighs.

He hears the rattling as Sweet Lucy Wine whips the roll of toilet paper, over and over. His butt begins to itch, and his nose, and sweat forms small beads where a mustache would be if he had one.

When he's sure he can't last any longer he hears the sound of her skin peeling away from the part of the seat Rafer McBride calls "the donut," and her feet pattering across the floor, then the cement, and up into her room.

When her door closes he eases out of the tub and sits on the edge. He takes a couple of deep breaths before he realizes Sweet Lucy Wine forgot to turn out the light. He also notices from the rancid smell she forgot to flush the commode. He doesn't know what he expected or was curious about, but it's not what it is. First he sees just color, the red and white, and then his eyes focus on the blobs of toilet paper and the blood.

He knows vaguely it's monthlies blood and no big deal—head truth—but that doesn't keep him from feeling the inside of his chest swell again, and heave. The smell of chickens boiling has finally seeped down to the basement, and it doesn't help him to get hit with that, either.

His hands begin a kind of wringing motion, as if he were squeezing a dishrag. They seem far away as he watches them, six miles below his stomach. They might be part of a TV show he could turn off and walk away from.

What is up close and inescapable is the awful explosion and lunging in his body. Anywhere else but here, he thinks, anybody else but me. A thick humming begins to rise in his chest. Nothing in the world could persuade him that this isn't his verdict. He's convinced he's about to be swallowed up.

Still, it's none of his doing, he realizes that, something in his throat tells him so, but it's not enough to keep the other thing in his throat from coming up, too, and he unloads his guts into the bowl with the blood and bones that he knows aren't bones, but you'd just as well tell that to the judge.

RAFER McBRIDE

I

HIS CHAIR

Rafer kept it in the alley that ran behind his house. Mark Random had never seen a piece of furniture so old, or so ugly. It was overstuffed, and what Rafer called its "innards" leaked out at various tears in the blotchy green covering.

Thumbtacked to the garage door behind it was a small, hand-lettered sign that used to say "Rafer's Chair." No one had bothered to take it down after the "Installation Ceremonies"; it was torn in half now, so only the first word was left. It disappeared when the garage door was up.

The one time Random had sat in the chair had been a shock, because the springs went through to the ground. It felt to him like stepping down when you think there're no more stairs but there are, and your foot plunges through the air where you thought floor was going to be, only by the time your brain gets *that* signal your foot *has* hit the floor.

That one time Random sat in it, however, was more than most people did. No one had ever heard Rafer actually say not to sit in it, but Random had noticed that if a bunch of them ever went by it on the way back from the movies or the store they would all look at it as if he had.

Of course, they'd all seen Rafer sit in it regularly, late on summer afternoons when the weather was nice, with the big garage door swung up behind him, like a man out in front of his cave. The way he fit into it, Random thought, settling down as if nothing could surprise him, was probably enough to make anyone realize what not to do.

Random thought the whole business with the chair was another way of knowing Rafer was inimitable. At least that was how he explained his amazement one July afternoon when he and Rafer found a stranger sitting in it.

They had come across Rafer's backyard, passed by the side of the garage, squeezed through the gate that had dug its bottom into the dirt, and started off down the alley to the movies when Rafer stopped. Random hadn't *seen* anything, but as soon as Rafer stopped he realized something off to the right was different, as if there were a thickness where there usually was a space.

They turned around. "Morning," Rafer said to the black man sitting in the chair. He was dressed in a midnight-blue, pinstripe suit. It was well worn in an unusual way, Random noticed, being shiny all over, not just at the places that get rubbed the most.

It was hard to tell how tall he was, but his bony knees stuck into the air so they seemed to make a triangle with his small head. His age was hard to guess, too, but to Random he seemed *old*—somewhere around ninety, he thought. But when he talked it was different.

"Un-hunh," he said. It was a deep, strong voice. It sounded to Random as if Rafer had made a judgment and the black man was agreeing with it.

"How you doing?" Rafer adjusted his body from its stopped position to one where he could listen without committing himself. It was a posture Random had seen him use before, although not often. The sunlight through the oak trees in the vacant lot across the alley flickered on the two of them. It looked as if someone were playing with a mirror. From the very beginning something seemed odd, but Random couldn't articulate it.

"Tollable." The black man spoke to Rafer, but he looked at where Rafer was standing rather than at Rafer himself. It didn't seem a challenge exactly, but it struck Random afterwards that Rafer was being asked to earn the space he filled up. Maybe that was what made him handle things the way he did.

"You?" the black man asked, inclining his head leftward slightly.

"Mobile," Rafer decided.

The black man smiled. "Sit down, then," he said. Random remembered his junior-high football coach's habit of walking up and down the sideline during scrimmages, yelling to the defensive linemen on every play, "Firm but loose, firm but loose." He'd never known exactly what that meant until he heard the black man in Rafer's chair use his voice.

"How 'bout some air first?" Rafer moved around behind the black man and heaved the garage door up. Random watched the little sign saying "Rafer's" snap up out of sight.

Even from where Random was standing he could feel a cold dampness drift past him. Some of the flecks of sunlight hit the dirt floor of the garage, black with grease and sludge drippings.

"There." Rafer rubbed his hands together as if he'd just made a fire and wanted to warm himself. Then he slid them two or three times against the sides of his khaki pants. He sat down on the gravel edge of the alley, Indian-style, making an L with the black man. For an instant Random had an image of them waiting for somebody else to show up for a card game.

The black man took his hands out of his lap and placed one on each knee, like the statue of Lincoln in Washington, D.C., except, Random thought, the living man was scrunched down in that funny way because of the chair.

"That your chair?" Rafer asked him.

The black man said, "Nope." He hitched himself a little, seeming almost to pop up into the air and back down. Then he ground his hands around on his kneecaps a couple of times.

"I was put here," he said.

"Un-hunh," Rafer said, looking off down the alley. Random was standing across from both of them and to one side; he looked where Rafer was looking. All he could see was the same old alley, empty, T-ing at Mr. Snoddy's garage four houses down.

"Put here," the black man echoed himself. His hands slid slowly down his thighs until they rested limply in his lap. His elbows stuck out across the arms of Rafer's chair. "Took um thirty years of pushin and draggin but they finely got me here this mornin. They overcame." He shook his little knob of a head two or three times—it looked to Random like an 8-ball rotating on a short pole.

"Who's that?" Rafer asked. His voice was matter-of-fact.

"It was like all the time I was fighten um I was wanten um to win, too. Buncha women, mostly—ants, wives, sisters—them kind. Bunch um."

He turned the last syllable into a hum that kept getting louder, making Random feel as if a train were coming toward him, until the man leaned his head back and opened his mouth and let the rest of it out in a great roar.

His head rested on the back of the chair then, and Random was surprised to see how big his Adam's apple was. It stuck out like a beak.

The loud roar seemed to go on up through the air as if it were made of something more solid than noise. Random was impressed at the way everything became quiet for a minute after that.

"Rafer," he said then, "come on. It's gonna be starting already." He kicked the crushed earth at the edge of his side of the alley.

"In a minute," Rafer said. His voice was still in neutral.

Random couldn't figure out why Rafer wanted to hang around any more. In fact, it didn't make any sense to him why Rafer hadn't told the old man whose chair it was right off and let it go at that. Either the old man was nuts or crazy, Random thought, and then realized suddenly he was afraid of him. He had a disturbing picture of that little round head popping off his neck and following his roar up into the air, like a cannonball.

Random picked up a rock and threw it past them into Rafer's garage.

Rafer stood up, rubbing his hands on his hips again. He didn't pay any more attention to Random than Adam did to God, but Random had to admit it wasn't all that unusual. Rafer could get hunkered down on the unlikeliest things.

"They coming after you?" Rafer asked. The black man's mouth hung open still and Rafer seemed to look down into it.

"Ahnn," the black man said, making Random think of the sound he made when the doctor pushed his tongue down to see his throat. The man's head seemed to return to normal, showing the same white holes where two tiny black disks floated for eyes. "Not so far as I know. They rode the part of me they liked best until it finely wore out. Can't see I got anything left to trade."

"Well," Rafer said, his voice sounding tighter than before, as if he'd squashed it together on itself, "this is your chair as long as you sit in it, I guess." He scuffed some gravel with his shoe. "Or until whoever owns it wants to sit in it and kicks you out." It was the only time Random ever heard Rafer talk as if he wasn't who he was.

"Come on," Rafer said, turning toward Random and starting down the alley. "Let's go to the movies."

They took a left at Mr. Snoddy's garage and emerged into McArthur Street. The next block and a half it seemed to Random as if he were walking beside a knot. Rafer had his head burrowed down in his neck. He snorted twice.

About a hundred feet from the movie he put his fingers on Random's arm and stopped them. "I couldn't make that man get out of my chair unless I'd helped put him into it in the first place, could I? And I can't see I had any part in that." He looked Random in the eye but Random knew he was really talking to himself.

Still, he seemed to relax some after that, and even joked about the Superman short, which he usually took seriously.

When they passed the chair on the way back from the movies,

the black man was gone. There was no way to tell he'd been there at all, Random thought, much less how long he'd sat after Rafer had talked with him.

Rafer and Random stopped for a second or two, and Random stared at the stains on the green covering. He had no way of knowing what Rafer looked at exactly, or what he thought, but from then on things seemed to change a little.

Rafer didn't quit sitting in the chair, but he sat in it less. And when he did, it seemed as if he were just visiting. He'd move on almost before he got comfortable. He never said anything about the whole business, either, to Random or, as far as Random knew, anyone else, but three or four of them commented at various times that they felt different walking past the chair when it was empty, less intimidated, almost as if some change had come over the chair itself. Then they would look sheepish at talking that way, reach down, pick up some gravel and throw it at the garage door.

No invitations were issued, but Random and a couple of Rafer's other friends began sitting down on occasion. After a while, the chair became something like a meeting place, especially, Random noticed, if someone had been getting flak from his mother, or his girl, or somebody else, and needed a place to talk about it, or just let it slide.

2

GIRLS

Mark Random hadn't known Rafer McBride long before he noticed that wherever Rafer went—to a dance, a ball game, even the cafeteria at lunch on a sunny day when you'd expect people to go outside after they'd finished eating—girls collected around him like filings around a magnet. Random knew they clustered around other boys—and sometimes himself, too, lately—but he could tell they wanted to make an impression, be sexy, or cool, or superior. But with Rafer it seemed different. They *listened* to Rafer. Some months passed before Random felt he could ask him why that happened.

"Cause of what I tell 'em," Rafer said.

"What's that?"

"Well," he said, "first I tell them how beautiful they are, and then I tell them how much I want them, and last I tell them another chapter in the history of Western civilization."

"Aw shit, Rafer," Random said. "Every time I ask you something serious you make a joke out of it."

They were sitting in the back seat of an old Nash Random's father couldn't let go of, even though the company had gone out of business. It was old enough to have horsehair seats that felt to Random in hot weather as if they'd wrap around him and suffocate him. His father, under pressure, had at least put seat covers on; they stuck to Random's skin only if he had shorts on. To his relief, that day had been indifferently hot and had cooled toward evening.

He and Rafer had been killing time playing what they called "pecker shapes." One of them would frog his legs out, stick his hand in his pants and arrange his penis and testicles, then take his hand out and press against his pants around the arrangement. Then the other one would do the same. The object was to make funny nonpecker shapes. They laughed a lot, but Random had to admit that mostly all they managed was different kinds of lumps.

He did notice, though, that Rafer's lumps were always a little larger than his, and he thought it must have been that that made him start thinking about Rafer and the girls, and get agitated when Rafer gave him that stuff about Western civilization.

Rafer looked at Random directly for perhaps as long as one gets to see a hummingbird in one place. Then he looked past him out the window.

"What is it you want to know exactly?" he said, his voice as thin and quiet as the sound thread makes when a needle takes it through cloth. One of Random's grandmothers used to say to him occasionally for no apparent reason that it wasn't the strength of the person sewing that mattered, it was the strength of the thread.

Random wasn't sure how to answer the question. He caught himself staring down at his hand inside his pants and pulled it out. For a second he seemed not to know what to do with it, watching it as if it were a little animal as unfamiliar and fascinating to him as his penis. Then he laid it across the back of the seat and made an effort to think.

Rafer shifted around so he was looking over the front seat out the windshield at the elm trees. Their leaves shuffled a little in the breeze, which wasn't strong enough to move into the car.

"You know how much my father likes to fish." It wasn't a question. It was common knowledge how Rafer's father would let whatever else slide if he could fix up a fishing trip. He was good at it, too. Random had heard the famous story about Rafer's father fishing from the same side of the boat with two other guys (or fifty, depending on how big the boat was) and while they sat there like pigeons on a rail he'd be pulling fish in like tomorrow was the last time.

"He can catch fish in a dry wash in July." Random couldn't tell from Rafer's voice if he admired that or was jealous of it, or both.

"Trouble is, he can't fish alone. He has to have company. Half the time it's female."

He looked over at Random again, not as intently as the first time, but longer. "Not many people know this, and how I know it doesn't matter, but he's had some regular fishing women for twenty, twenty-five years." He looked back out the windshield, and went on in the same voice. "One at a time, I mean, but not one of 'em's been my mother."

Rafer was sitting on the curb side of the car. He opened his door. The bottom scraping on the dirt sounded like something tearing, but some of the breeze started coming in, which felt good to him. It was getting dark.

"I don't know where they stay when they aren't fishing with him, but I do know this, for a fact. Fishing is *all* they do with him. And talk. No matter how the fishing goes they always talk. Goes out in that boat all day till it's so dark mullets would jump to a flashlight, and comes in and takes her home like he was on a first date.

"I've seen a couple of 'em, never mind how." Rafer's voice softened, taking on the tone he'd used to tell Random about the pass he'd intercepted to win the Hampton game the previous fall. "Big women, I mean not fat but tall, filled out just right. One of 'em was loud, too—talked like she ate gravel and it tasted good. I heard her tell my father a joke, and it—" He broke off, laughing.

"I never saw them in the boat, but I bet they slid that worm on the hook as smooth as Vaseline." The last of his laughter trailed off. Even though it didn't seem all that hot to Random, a cicada started its metallic gargling noise in one of the elms.

"And you know my mother," Rafer said, sounding like he was sharpening a knife. "All the time drawing her mouth flat, smelling like a perfume factory in the morning, making us eat on those fancy plates at dinner. And color-coordinated, Lord, I bet her diapers were color-coordinated." The way he stopped sounded as if he had a lot more to say, but all he did was start shaking his head slowly back and forth. Then he leaned forward and rested it on the top edge of the front seat.

"From what I can tell my father has never been able to get his fishing woman and his fucking woman to be the same." His voice went down toward the floor, but each word was as clear as a firefly lighting up. "And he must've done a lot of fishing before he married my mother."

His forehead made a sticky noise as he lifted it from the seat cover and leaned back. He breathed out and laughed at once.

Slumping down in the seat, he propped his feet through the window hole of the open door.

"There's that," he said, blowing his breath out again, like a runner getting his lungs clear. "And there's this: the ones I know all seem to believe in the barter system. So far."

"Hunh," Random interrupted. "I know this isn't a very big contribution to the conversation, but ones what?"

"What we're talking about. What you asked me about. Girls. I think most of them don't even know they believe in it, unless playing innocent's a bigger deal than I thought."

"I think you lost me somewhere on the fishing trips," Random said. He felt an impulse to go in the house and watch TV, but he realized there was nothing much he liked on in the summer— comedy programs he never found funny, family shows too perfect to believe. *Bore-ore-oring*, he thought and noticed Rafer was chuckling again. It didn't seem to bother Random that part of it might have been aimed at him.

"It doesn't matter," Rafer said. "You'll catch on when you need to." He looked out the window beside Random, a puzzled expression on his face. "Maybe it comes natural to them, in the genes," he said, as if he couldn't believe himself. "Like animals that do all that stuff without ever being taught any of it. Birds, and flies," he said, a smile spreading his mouth out. "Rabbits." He laughed out loud again.

"Rafer," Random said, opening his door and getting out, "I'm gonna fetch the keys to this heap and we'll go get some DQ."

"Yeah. Right." Rafer laughed harder still. "I'll have a cherry sundae."

Random thought that was a cheap one, but it turned out to be exactly what Rafer ordered. On the way over in the car he didn't say anything, although he made some grunting noises when Random asked him about his construction job.

Random didn't talk a lot either. He realized that while Rafer had been talking he had begun to feel as if the car were sealed up like a submarine. Now he enjoyed feeling the wind cutting in the windows, tousling his hair.

He thought about Sweet Lucy Wine, still living in his grandmother's house and carrying on an independent life. She made even the smallest motion appear to be performed with such incredible ease. In spite of his jealousy of his brother, he saw Sweet Lucy Wine reach out and welcome Luke in the swing, smiling, talking inaudibly like a river to its banks, making Luke smile in return. She could have been there in the car, he saw her so clearly. Most of the time he wanted to be Luke so he could be in her arms—there was no point denying that—but as he drove he realized for a second or two in his imagining that he was himself in her arms. No substitute, no kin between him and her enfolding warmth. All this in spite of what he tried not to remember about her and Mr. Mann.

Until now she had seemed mysterious, and the girls at his high school known, people whose beings he could have described as easily as the rings in a tree stump. But now it seemed turned upside down, and Sweet Lucy Wine became the one he knew, although he had no words for his knowledge.

He had an urge to dump Rafer and go home. For the first time he wanted to talk to Sweet Lucy Wine, ask her questions about herself.

But he drove on, the breeze stirring the heat out of the old Nash. He turned at Malvern onto Broad, ignoring the amber light as it switched to red. As they parked next to the picnic tables in front of the Dairy Queen, Random noticed the little red bulbs in the Q were blinking, as if they were about to go out. No one else was there so he and Rafer got their order right away. Rafer didn't flirt with the girl behind the window with the porthole.

Random watched as Rafer ate his DQ on what he called "the installment plan"—he would get a big load on the white plastic spoon, put it in his mouth, and not quite close his lips when he pulled it out, so he had a mound left on the spoon. He'd gradually decrease his mouth opening and manage to get eight or nine installments from one spoonful. Random contented himself with a double chocolate cone.

Rafer attacked his sundae and said, "They're always looking to find out what you've got to trade for it. I haven't found any exceptions yet, either." While he cleaned a last installment off his spoon, digging down with his top lip, Random decided he must be talking about what he'd called the barter system. "Not even Teddygirl Hardin." He did his eyebrows up and down, reminding Random of Groucho Marx. "They *never* give it away.

"I figure the best way to handle that is to get 'em to start listening to you. Messes up their antennae. If I can get them to listen— I mean actually *listen*—to the words I'm saying, they get mixed up about where the signals are coming from. Or if there are any. They watch my mouth, or my hands, or some other part of my body, because the sounds they're hearing don't seem to have anything to do with what they expected."

He scooped another spoonful of his sundae, which had already begun to resemble liquid chalk. The cherry juice ran off like oil off water.

"Nothing confuses them like talk does. Especially about civilization. They eventually have to hang onto my words intently because they're trying to figure out what I have that they want badly enough to get me interested in trading for it.

"But the real confusion develops when I don't make any offers. They start to wonder what's wrong then, because I don't act like what they've got is worth trading for, or even like trading exists." He took a large installment and said around it, "It isn't exactly like dogs sniffing each other's behinds, but it isn't exactly not, either."

He worked the mouthful down slowly. "The thing is," he said thickly, "is not to get where they can lead you around by the nose."

He stared off into the street a minute, working on his sundae. Between installments he smiled at Random and said, "Of course, I don't turn it down, you understand."

"So I hear," Random said.

Rafer's smile froze for a second. "You don't usually listen to me like this. You taken up with somebody? Angie Thompson? Beverly Cole? Who is it? Somebody I don't know?"

Even before Rafer asked him those questions, Random had been getting restless again. But he surprised himself by saying, "No. Nobody in particular." That didn't sound right to him, so he said, "Everybody." That didn't sound right either.

"What I mean is everybody seems the same—Cynthia Reynolds equals Millie Severson equals Wanda Katz equals everybody. One of them melts into the next one when I try to think about who they are." He had an image of Rafer's father multiplied by fifty—fifty Mr. McBrides lined up along the side of a big trawler, their rods over the edge, fishing in a bay without water. "Shit, Rafer, they're all gonna grow up to be your mother."

He paid no attention to Rafer's reaction, but sat there staring past him at the Dairy Queen curl on the neon sign above him. Pigtail. When Sweet Lucy Wine's hair had been long he'd watched her braid it while she looked at the TV. Her fingers had fascinated him, rolling the black ropes of hair, twining them one over the other, separate, in control. Remembering their motion now made his stomach feel like silk rustling.

"Leave it be," he said to Rafer, wiping his mouth with a paper napkin. He looked at the inch or so of empty cone left in his hand and punched his thumb into it.

Rafer had stopped badgering him and said something Random didn't quite hear about a few of the girls hanging around after he'd finished talking because they couldn't figure out what they'd gotten, if anything.

Random stood up and crunched the empty water cups and the rest of his cone and napkin into a pile between his hands, walked over, and stuffed them into the trash can. It had a dome top with a swinging flap, and nearly caught his finger when it sprang back.

"Damn," he said, coming back to the table, standing there with his hands on his hips. He felt as if he had more to say but a lot of it seemed to involve Rafer's mother, or his own. All that came out was, "Sometimes you make me mad."

"Yeah," Rafer said. "You've got *something* on your mind. Maybe you're frustrated by what I left out. That part's easy—to say, I mean—but hard to bring off. If you accept the system all you've really got to trade is your self. A way out of that is not to accept the system, which maybe I don't. I'm not sure."

A breeze jostled the sundae container, and he had to juggle it to keep it balanced in his hands.

"I'm never sure. I'm always hiding something. I feel like my old man must sometimes, shut out on both sides where there ought to be a joining. Having to work on something that feels like it wants to come naturally."

He looked at Random, all suggestion of amusement or superiority gone, at least for the moment.

"I think about that all the time—protecting what I want to give away. You may be right—maybe they *will* all grow up to be our mothers. But I sure hate to admit it. It makes the future look like the wrong side of the boat."

He pushed the dome flap back with his left hand and dropped the trash into the hole with his right. When he let go, the flap swung back and forth cleanly three or four times.

3

HIS MOTHER

"Rafer, Rafer, Rafer," she would say, as if she were apologizing for something, or making a wish. When Rafer's mother would call off his name it would sound to Random like a totem pole looked, one name stacked on top of another and on up until the thing was tall enough to fall over if pushed in the right place.

She would say his name three or four times with different

pauses for different occasions and then, as often as not, if Rafer and Random were in the house, pull aside a curtain and look at the picture window. Random always thought it was an act. They were supposed to think she was seeing something outdoors, but he didn't believe it. Spanking clean glass always, but as far as he could tell she never really looked through it. When she turned back toward them she would have a glazed look in her eyes.

Then she would head out the front door with her purse on her arm, climb in the new Fleetwood and drive off. Just before she flipped the gearshift into drive she would fluff her colored hair out behind her neck and glance up into the rearview mirror. From the window Random could see her readjusting it as she went off down the street.

"Takin' off," Rafer would say, not so much to Random, or anybody else who might be there, as to the curtain, which would be still swaying a little as it settled into itself by the window. "Let's go get some peanut butter," he'd say, and be in the kitchen before Random realized he'd moved. Random marveled at Rafer's quickness; it was the kind that made him such a good halfback, slippery as an egg white, big tackles wondering where he'd been.

He would be spreading the Peter Pan Smooth on crackers with a spoon handle by the time Random got to the formica table with the tube legs in the kitchen.

"What we gone do with 'em today?" Rafer would ask. It was a ritual question.

"I don't know," Random would say.

Rafer was referring to their mothers, but Random never knew exactly what he might be thinking. The procedure was his invention anyway, coming up with some new torture or inconvenience for their mothers. Random always felt a little uncomfortable about it, too; he became slow to take Rafer up on the peanut butter after a while. But he had to admit Rafer's game gave him a kind of satisfaction.

"Put 'em in a room," Rafer said once. The cracker he was

pushing the peanut butter onto snapped and started to jackknife between his fingers. He tilted his hand and let it slide onto the table.

Random was standing with his hand on the back of a kitchen chair, the kind that folds up, looking out the six long glass panels on the porch door.

"They would have straight chairs they would sit up straight in. Purple walls with pink flowers on them—and a yellow ceiling." The waxy paper in the box crinkled as he got another cracker. "No. Chartreuse."

Random could see Rafer's head turn toward him in his peripheral vision, but he knew from the past Rafer wasn't looking at him. So he kept his eyes on the backyard. Nothing was happening.

"Right. Your mother can have a banana," Rafer said. Then he reconsidered. "No, a peach. It's a peach she's got, a fuzzy, ripe peach. She peels it very slowly. In *my* mother's face." He said those words as deliberately as if he were himself peeling the peach, a word for each section of the skin coming off.

"And my mother has to keep her hands in her lap. Can't touch it. Can't take a bite."

Random looked down at him. The spoon handle was buried in a glob of peanut butter, suspended on its way to the cracker in his other hand. He seemed to be staring at the space between.

"And you know what? It's gonna be that when your mother gets it peeled, all that extra juice sliding through her fingers down to her elbow making her queasy, she's not gonna know what to do with it." He sounded to Random as if he'd discovered space flight, or jacking off. His eyes focused and he smiled all over his face. He looked at Random.

"My mother is gone have to watch your mother sit there, holding that peach like she's waiting for a rainbow to grow out of it." He stuck the glob of peanut butter into his mouth and sucked it off the spoon handle. "Let's go throw some ball," he said in his normal voice. He handed Random the empty cracker and was gone looking for his glove.

Sometimes Rafer's mother would count off his name because he'd done something she had to discipline him about. When that happened she'd stay in the house, not drive off in the Caddy. Random could tell what was going on because she would stay away from the window. She would walk around the living room, like a caged wazoo, as Rafer put it.

Rafer would either stand by the piano at the back, which meant she would pass close by him once every time around, or move along across from her, keeping the same distance between them all the time, which seemed to Random like a pony and a trainer without a rope. Or with an invisible one.

Whenever she got close to Rafer it looked to Random as if she were going to chew him up, so Random asked him once why he *ever* stood still by the piano. "Because," Rafer said, "that way there's a second or two each circle where she can't look at me. And then it seems for another second or two like she's walking away." He smiled. "You take your small favors, don't you know?"

Small favors, Random thought. He guessed his was that he'd usually get sent to the kitchen when he was there for one of those tussles. Other times he'd stand in the doorway to the screened porch. He knew that where he was when the ruckus started determined whether he'd just get to listen, or have to watch, too.

It was some relief to him never to be actually in the arena, although the screened porch doorway was too close for the All Night Necking Blow-Up. Any place would've been too close for that one, he thought; it had to be the worst. You'd have thought Rafer had committed grand larceny on Wiley Drug and murdered the pope.

The football team had beaten Northside Friday night. Rafer had scored two touchdowns and had given Northside's all-conference split end a hard time on pass reception. "Raked the beejesus out of him," Random had said proudly to Rafer afterwards. "Poor guy got so when he'd see the ball coming toward him in the air he'd hear a herd of bulls coming up behind on the ground." He had dropped three passes by the time the coach took him out of the game in the middle of the third quarter.

A good night on defense would set Rafer up. Random had seen him outside the locker room with Mini Rotho Lamb, the head cheerleader, whose nickname derived from her skirt length, and it turned out they'd spent most of the night up at Boyster's Dam, parked in Mini's T-bird. Rafer told Random later it was worth all the noise mostly, but allowed it would have been in his interest to have gotten her home before 4 A.M.

It was about ten o'clock Saturday morning when Random arrived at the McBrides' front door. He walked in as he always did. Rafer and his mother were in the middle of it already.

"You get over there and mind your business," Rafer's mother said to Random. Her voice sounded to him as if it went from her teeth to her throat to her teeth as it moved along the sentence, as if she were trying to be polite to him somewhere in the middle of it.

Over there meant the screened-porch doorway, where Random went.

"Smartass handjob," she hissed at Rafer, who was standing by the piano.

She had her nightshift buttoned crooked so a flap of it fell away from her neck. Random wouldn't call her Jane Russell, but she didn't have anything to complain about either. She had her rings and bracelets and earrings on, and lipstick and eye makeup. And magenta curlers in her dyed hair. To Random it was a disconcerting assortment of different things bouncing and jiggling while she went through her head thrusting and finger jerking at Rafer.

She didn't exactly yell at him. Her voice made Random imagine a snake's hissing combined with the sound a file would make if you dragged it through a hole just tight enough on it to grate. She was mad.

"You could have *told* me you had a date. Or called after the game." She gritted her teeth. "You have no idea how I worry about you when I don't know where you are. Don't you know

Boyster's Dam is a hoodlum hangout? Didn't you care just a *little* about what's-her-name? She could've been raped up there."

She stood at the coffee table, her hands fluttering around on her stomach and then beside her hips. She reached down into the silver box and snatched out a cigarette. While she was bent over she kept watching Rafer at the other end of the room by the piano. Random thought for an instant he was watching one of those Western movies and she was afraid Rafer would draw on her.

She flicked the table lighter, a hunk of silver in her hand, coaxing out a tiny flame. She lit the cigarette, took a short drag on it, put the lighter down so it hit the cigarette box and fell over, and then pointed the cigarette at Rafer. Smoke came out of her mouth when she talked.

"I don't care how big a hotshot you are on that football team, you're going to pay for this little escapade where it hurts you the most." Her eyes glazed over and she bobbed the cigarette up and down.

"I don't know how yet, but I'll come up with something appropriate by supper."

That word seemed to light up her eyes. "I'll tell you one thing. Tonight you stay home. In that room." Her cigarette arm pointed at the ceiling as if she were the Statue of Liberty. "No TV, no radio, no nothing. And tomorrow."

She stopped, but Random could tell she wasn't through. She smoked some more, her other hand fiddling with the knot in the sash around the middle of her shift. For a second Random had the disquieting feeling that she wanted to take it off.

He looked down the room at Rafer, who had on what he called his Withdrawn Expression. "The object," he'd once told Random, "is to *look* empty, like all she says is pouring in, like I almost want her to chew me out. She runs down quicker on the withdrawn face than on any other. Mistakes it for shamefulness, I think."

After his mother had dragged her cigarette down almost to

the filter, a twitch ran through her torso and she noticed Random was still there. She looked at him as if he might have been an extension of Rafer. She moved around to the couch behind the coffee table and sat down. When she jammed the cigarette filter into the ashtray, one of her fingernails speared it and it split open, revealing the ragged, white fibers.

The tip of her tongue showed between her lips and she made a small *tppppting* sound as if trying to get something off of it. "You can have company till after lunch, but that's it." She rubbed her hands down her thighs on the shiny material of the shift, twice. Then she looked up at Rafer.

He hadn't moved from the piano. Random noticed his Withdrawn Expression had faded; his face looked harder and his eyes seemed to have shrunk in on themselves. Although he wasn't in the stance he took on defense, he looked as if his body were thinking about it, beginning to tense somewhere inside as if an alarm were about to sound which only Rafer could hear.

His right arm began to rise from his side, slowly, when his mother started up again.

"Goddamn electric monotony middle age—" She cut herself off as if someone had unplugged her. Then she picked up again as if nothing had happened. "—teenage arrogant big-balled switchy-titchy—" Another sudden break. Random almost expected a commercial. "—high-and-mighty crotch poker ride God knows I thought—" another break. "—God knows what I thought."

And she spurted from the couch out into the hall and up the stairs.

Rafer had explained to Random once that his mother's tirades had four parts. The first was the countdown on his name, surrounded by deep looks and heavy silences. Then came what he called "the launch," an incoherent ramble that he described as a combination of calls on unseen powers to explain why she was visited with such a plague, and curses of a general kind directed at him for being in the world at all. It was the longest. He said they were the only times he thought his mother was interesting. Random himself had heard her get uncomfortably raunchy in phase two.

Rafer presented phase three as "a lot of shit about responsibility and cooperation," during which she smoked incessantly. With four came The Sentence. "She hasn't hooked the sentence into the crime right yet," he'd said. "Always uses some little-boy knuckle-slapper, like sending me to my room. If I was half the stuff she says I am when she's mad, she'd have to send me to Devil's Island."

It was evident to Random that today he had walked in on the last bit of phase two. It was equally evident it had been the most pee-tuckering phase two yet, because after Rafer's mother went back upstairs to dress, Rafer took an unusual tack.

Random was used to Rafer's telling him things that sounded personal but that always ended up being philosophy, layered over two or three times like the inside of a baseball. The center was never anything like the covering he'd gone through to get there.

But this time to his surprise it seemed to be genuine stuff, which was almost as odd as noticing that something in Rafer's voice reminded him of his own mother. Random wasn't sure what it was exactly—a sound, perhaps, of having to do one thing when you'd give your eyeteeth to do another.

"I wonder if the woman knows what she wants," Rafer said. He said it to Random, but he was looking out the front window behind the couch. "You missed the good part. She spent a half hour inventing ways of telling me *I* was a pervert."

For the first time since his mother had lit her cigarette he moved, finished the motion he'd started with his right arm, scratching his forehead, shifting his weight to one leg so his hip was off kilter. It might have been taken as a small easing of the tension in his body, but to Random it was more a misdirection, as if Rafer were postponing something he wasn't sure about. Random wasn't sure what his position meant, either, since he no longer felt like a spectator.

"I shouldn't be surprised she has an imagination like that. I spent part of an afternoon once going through the old man's chest of drawers, and I saw how big his rubbers are." His gaze passed over Random's on the way to the fireplace, where it settled. "You know what that makes her."

He shifted his weight to the other leg and cleared his throat.

"You don't have to be God to know what goes on up there. Or even very smart." He made a burst of sound Random supposed was a laugh, until it modulated into an imitation of the whiny chuckling of the announcer on "The Shadow" who said, *"Who knows what evil lurks in the hearts of men?"*

"The walls are thin," Rafer said, stretching the chuckling out to cover his words. "And the natives are restless."

He had raised both hands as he spoke and didn't seem to know what to do with them. He brought them together gently against the sides of his head, making cups over his ears. He turned half around and leaned on the piano.

"Ah, hell," he said, so softly Random had to strain to hear him. "Maybe she's right. I don't know. Maybe the whole thing is just one long prophylactic stretched from here to kingdom come, and the lucky ones don't slip out through the leaks." It was barely a whisper.

Rafer lowered his arms, turning his head toward Random, slitting his eyes. "What do you think?" he said, his voice neutral again, skating on the surface of things, suddenly loud in the still room.

Random wasn't sure it was a real question or, if it was, whether Rafer wanted an answer, so he said nothing.

Rafer turned away from the piano, looked at the ceiling, ran the tip of his tongue up under his top lip. "It's not fishing, that's for sure," he said, letting his eyes drift down until he was looking at Random, only he wasn't. "And it's not a game."

He eased his arms across each other slowly, hugging himself.

He raised his eyebrows slightly and then lowered them, looking away from Random.

Suddenly, without seeming to move, he was facing Random in the defensive stance Random had half-expected him to assume before his mother's final, broken outburst—body poised, arms slightly circled, weight tilted forward on the balls of his feet. A low growl collected in his throat, a sound it seemed the whole world might be able to center on.

Before Random could get out of the way Rafer charged him. Random fell backwards into the couch, his left shin slipping under the coffee table and cracking against its edge.

He watched as Rafer cut ninety degrees left a foot in front of where he had been standing and disappeared into the dining room. He sat up and rubbed his shin, hearing through Rafer's shivering laughter a cabinet door in the kitchen open. He expected to hear as well the sound of the top spinning off the Peter Pan Smooth, but it didn't happen. Instead the back door opened, and the screen door to the porch slammed shut seconds later.

Random imagined the two doors—one a larger version of the other except for the glass panels—angling open into the square spaces of the kitchen, and Rafer, infinitesimally netted by the back porch screen, walking away.

4

PLAYING TOUCH

It was one of those long passes that looked as if it would hang in the sky all weekend. The spiral was a little off-center, a dog walking with a limp, but Ned Grim had laid it out on a dead line with the curb, and that was what mattered.

If a long pass was thrown in the middle of the median, or even somewhat to either side, all the defender had to do was just get in the way a little, keep from tripping over his own feet, and most of the time he would get a piece of the ball and knock it away. But if the receiver ran along the edge of the median, and the passer threw the ball on a line with the curb, or better still just a little bit outside it in the street, then there was no way anyone could bat it down.

The receiver would do his tightrope run along the curb, reach out when the ball floated down, tuck it under his arm, and that was that. Six, easy, Random thought, nothing you could do about it.

The trouble was, Rafer McBride had seen this one coming and was trying to repeat the only defensive maneuver that Random had seen work against what they called "the deep sideline bomb."

Random watched as Rafer dropped back and let Lord Jack Hart get up a full head of steam trying to run under Ned Grim's wobbly spiral. Rafer's plan was to arrive at the spot the catch would be made a split second ahead of Lord Jack, leap out over the street and knock the ball down in one motion as Lord Jack thundered by, empty-handed. Then he would let his body complete the spin it had started, and land gracefully, still running, on the pavement. Random had seen Rafer accomplish similar stunts at the stadium in real games.

But here it was more difficult, since the rules said the defender had to hit the ball before he stepped into the street. And this time Random figured it was nearly impossible because of the particular circumstances. First, knocking a pass loose from Lord Jack, even for Rafer, was about as easy as slipping the sunrise past a rooster, and second, Rafer's timing was off.

He got there an instant too late and Lord Jack ran over him. Random thought the thud and the sound of Rafer sucking wind could have been heard at the Fairgrounds.

Rafer curled up into a ball, reminding Random of one of those roly-poly bugs he sometimes found under the sink. After a minute his body pried itself apart, his legs groping out into the street so the top part of his body was on the grass of the median and his bottom half stuck out onto the asphalt. The curb cut him in half under his back.

All the players stood and watched. It was dead quiet the way it gets whenever something unexpected happens. It wasn't unusual for people to bump each other around playing football on the median dividing the street in front of the McBrides' house. It was only twelve feet wide, so in a couple of hours' normal routine on Saturday afternoon some of them always ended up with their share of skins and bruises. But nobody had gotten really laid out like this.

So when Rafer went down all balled up everyone froze. Except Lord Jack. His pushing Ned Grim out of the way in the cluster of people around Rafer broke the spell. When Ned stumbled, Random looked past him over his shoulder and saw the football like a big brown egg in the grass three houses down, where the goal had been marked.

Random concluded that Lord Jack must have kept on going after he'd run through Rafer, put the ball down to prove that he had scored, and then sprinted back.

When Random turned his head back to the group, Lord Jack had pulled Rafer all the way up on the grass. Rafer was lying on his back, still as a dime.

Lord Jack unhooked Rafer's belt two notches and hooked it up again. He unsnapped Rafer's jeans and pulled the fly zipper down halfway.

It seemed to Random as if Rafer weren't looking at Lord Jack at all, but past his head into the sky. Random had seen guys get their wind knocked out before, but their faces hadn't looked like Rafer's. His didn't seem panicked at all, just gathered up, ready for something.

Lord Jack straddled Rafer, put his fingers inside the top of Rafer's jeans. As he started to lift up on them, a car—to Random's astonishment an old Model T—came chugging around the corner. It swerved toward the house-side curb and then came back toward the median at an angle. It eased the left front tire up over the curb and onto the grass, straightened out, and brought half the rear end up there, too.

Random had to look over and through Lord Jack and Rafer to see the car, and when he remembered the incident later it seemed as if a number of things had happened at once, suspended for an instant, as between lightning and thunder.

First were the tires like sticks on each side of the car's grille, and the car itself letting out its unmistakable, inimitable sound— *ooogah, ooogah.*

Then the discovery of who was driving—Wonderbuns, smiling as if she had just invented everybody. She seemed huge, sitting up there behind the wheel, looking down on them like an engineer in a train. The grass and some of the players reflected faintly over her smile in the windshield, and the sun hit off its metal edge.

Then seeing Rafer grab Lord Jack's hands the fraction of a second before Lord Jack could lift up on his jeans. He looked Lord Jack in the eyes, and, as Random thought later, the hardness that took over might have been what he had been preparing for.

The only sound for all that was the horn, and its fading into the air.

Then everything broke loose, as it always does. Stinky Naughton and Ned Grim and a couple of others went over to the car and got on it and in it. The motor was sputtering and coughing. Wonderbuns shook her hair off of her forehead and yelled to Lord Jack to come on and go for a ride in this thing, you could feel it shake your teeth. Random thought, Maybe she's not really smiling. Lord Jack turned his head first toward Wonderbuns, then toward Rafer, looking blank, not so much undecided as overcome. Rafer never took his eyes off Lord Jack, and Random couldn't tell if he was holding onto Lord Jack's hands to keep him from pulling or to make him pay attention to what was happening.

Jack let go and straightened up. He hitched his own pants. He looked down at Rafer, then past Random down the median as if he were a surveyor sighting on something. Then he lifted his left leg over Rafer, walked to the Model T, and got in on the shotgun side.

Wonderbuns scraped the car into gear and started off.

Random turned as they passed, and watched them drive away, one side on the median, one side on the street, the high cab of the Model T tilted toward the row of houses on the right.

When they passed the football still in the bright grass where Lord Jack had laid it, Random heard Rafer's voice behind him calling, "Hey Jack, don't sqush them peaches," and the sound of his laughter echoing through the hollow afternoon.

STRAWBERRY HILL

Mark Random wanted some air. He slid off the arm of the over-stuffed chair, slipped between two forms just before they merged into one, maneuvered through the rest of the crowd, and stood in the doorway to the next room. The sound of the bottle clinking and spinning, muffled as it was by the people clustered around it, already seemed far away.

He took two or three deep breaths, easing the cramped, stale feeling inside his chest. He pulled his crumpled handkerchief out of his pocket and scrubbed his lips, then stuffed it back in without looking at it. He was about to cross the empty room to go outdoors, maybe leave the place altogether, but a sudden commotion made him turn around and peer back into the smoky dimness.

The crowd stirred and parted, and two forms, a shorter one pulling a taller one after it, emerged. Random recognized Benny Codbill, and then Edith Madden, one of the two or three most desirable girls at the party.

"Come on, Edie," Codbill was saying, dragging her toward the doorway where Random stood. "This is *my* kiss, not Streater's or Burns's. I played the game the same way they did, and you owe *me*."

The way Codbill's words seemed to tumble out of his smile reminded Random of jelly beans coming out of the toy clown's mouth at the fair.

"Don't matter what you *want*," he said as they passed Random in the doorway, the belt buckle on his puffy stomach scraping Random's thigh. Random was surprised at his impulse to spit on Codbill's slicked-down hair; if I'd had an oyster ready, he thought, I could've laid it right in the part.

He turned and watched Codbill cross the room, making Edith trip on the old rug wrinkling on the cement floor. She hadn't quite gotten her balance back when Codbill started up the stairs and suddenly stopped on the second step. She was still trying to catch her feet up with the rest of herself, tipped forward, and just as Codbill turned around her foot snagged on the bottom step and she fell into him.

Random couldn't see everything that happened, the lights being dim to start with, and mostly red and blue through the paper hung on the bulbs, but in the instant Codbill turned around he'd seen his eyes squint shut and his round lips get rounder, puckering. Then Edith was standing on the floor two steps below him, looking him in the eye.

"That counts," she said, pulling her shirt sleeve out even with her sweater sleeve on the arm Codbill had been holding.

"Don't," Benny Codbill said. He wiped his left cheek with the back of his left hand. Then he held his hand in front of him and looked at it as if he had discovered an animal with a part missing. For a long minute Random watched him stare at Edith Madden really hard, as if he wanted to shoot something at her with his eyes. "You might think you can pull that cheek shit on Dickie Truffer," he said. "But not on me. Come here."

He reached out to pull her to him again. The way the lights hit his eyes made them gleam like targets, the kind at the shooting gallery at the fair, Random thought, that spin so fast they could hypnotize Houdini. Then Codbill's mouth popped open and a deep pig noise spurted out when Edith grabbed his left arm and jerked him off the steps.

He fell and rolled over the rug, making it bunch up under him.

Edith Madden stood over him, hands on hips. "I don't care if you are older than us, you don't get to be king. Or talk trash like that, either."

Random had never seen her mad, but standing there yelling at Codbill she seemed to be filled up with it, like she breathed it in and it stayed inside her. She didn't exactly remind Random of his mother, whom he saw as permanently skinny with her anger, like a bullwhip, but they both sounded the same—as if they could pick your peaches with their voice, he thought. He rubbed his right hand on his thigh. Too much of that and you could kiss your future family good-bye.

Codbill seemed not to expect what he got, either. He stared up at Edith Madden. His round body seemed to have shrunk in on itself, and his face had gone so flat it looked as if somebody had painted it on the front of his head. Random realized he never would have expected that could happen to someone like Codbill. For a moment he felt sympathy for the guy, which surprised him.

Edith had her body set as if she might spit on Codbill, but she didn't. Then she let her left hand loose from her hip and it hung down by her side. Her voice got lower. "I don't know who invited you here, Toad," she said, "but I bet nobody did. Why is it you hang around us, anyhow?"

About the time she called him a freak somebody pushed Random from behind, hard. He shot out into the room, tripped on the bunched-up side of the rug, and fell into Benny Codbill.

Codbill had gotten up on all fours, so that after Random fell and rolled a little on his side, he was looking up at an odd angle into Codbill's face. The lights above Codbill's head made him seem to glow blue and red around the edges, and his dark face was like a tunnel. Random could see the end of his nose glinting, protruding out of the blackness toward him far enough to catch the glow from Mrs. Truffer's flashlight. She had marched down the stairs, making noises none of Random's crowd liked to hear anytime, much less at a party. They always ask *What's going on?* he thought, as if it was wrong no matter what it was.

She shone the big spot on Random and Codbill while they got

up off the floor and brushed themselves off. Random was grateful to her for keeping it out of their eyes—she shone it mostly on their chests and belts, which he appreciated since he never knew how to look when he got caught at something, even when he wasn't doing anything he'd be ashamed of being caught at.

Evidently she decided there wasn't anything worth carrying on about. She made some small talk with Edith Madden, smiling vaguely. She looked over at the two or three people crowded in the doorway to the bottle room, where it had gotten very quiet. Then she pushed her hair off her cheek and went back upstairs, her arm at her side, the flashlight swinging its beam on the steps beside her like another set of feet.

Codbill and Random were standing beside each other in the middle of the rug, as if stranded on an island. Random heard some shuffling and looked over toward the door to the bottle room. It was empty. He thought Edith Madden had probably slipped in there again, but he couldn't be sure. It seemed to him unlikely she'd followed Mrs. Truffer upstairs.

"You going back in there?" Codbill said.

It took Random a second to notice he was the only person Codbill could be talking to.

"I don't know," he said.

The blue and red streamers looked dingy to him all of a sudden; the creases in the crepe paper seemed full of little specks of black grit. He felt if he stood in the rug much longer it would start wiggling and curl up and swallow him, as if he were in a horror movie. He stepped off of it.

"No," he said.

"Me neither," Codbill said. "Bunch of hoidytoidy shits. Miz Highbrow and all the Clean Jeans." He stuck his hand in his crotch and pulled at his undershorts. "Wouldn't know a pecker from birdshit. Come on."

He stepped off the other side of the rug and walked over to the outside door, the wooden part of which was ajar. The spring on the screen croaked when he pushed it open.

"Come on," he said again.

Random went out, letting the door slam, and shutting the big door, too.

Codbill had his car started before Random got halfway up the Truffers' slanted front yard. He reached over and pushed open the door for Random; it came all the way out and started to swing back shut. Random caught it on the bounce, just before it slammed shut again.

"Where we going?" he said through the window.

"Going to the fair," Codbill said. "To the Stet Fair." Random noticed the odd pronunciation, but even so he thought the fair sounded better than going home, or where he'd been, so he got in.

Codbill hit all the lights going out Viburnum to the Fairgrounds, driving to beat hell, until he pulled up at the double red lights at the entrance intersection.

Random had been holding tightly to the door pull. He let go and looked over at Codbill. The red and yellow lights strung up over the intersection and down the entranceway into the fair were swinging in the breeze, and they made a shifting shine on Codbill's cheek and the side of his mouth, like water on ice.

"I love that sign," Codbill said, pointing up above the gates to the Fairgrounds and racing his motor. The big red letters said STRAWBERRY HILL against a yellow background.

"I found my thrill," he said, and made a sound more like a snort than a laugh. One of the reds switched to a green arrow and Codbill turned toward Random. "You ever see a strawberry hill?"

The look in his eyes made Random feel suddenly as if Codbill knew a secret about him. That wasn't in itself troubling. What bothered him was his own feeling that he had the same secret only he didn't know what it was. He wondered if that was the way Codbill had looked at Edith Madden on the steps.

"No," Codbill said, "course you haven't," and looked back to the lights as they turned double green.

He peeled across the intersection, pulled into a parking place that had just opened up, and shut off the engine. "Most people," he said, "would think it was a hill with strawberries growing on it. And then they'd be not so many who would think you were asking a trick question and say it was a hill made out of a strawberry."

He snorted again. With the first finger on his right hand he was flipping the keys still hanging in the ignition. They'd swing back and forth a few times and stop, and he'd flick them again. From Random's side he could see Codbill's face squinch up like he was smiling. "Which ain't all that far off, come to think of it. But it ain't right, neither."

He rolled his little body around so his right leg came up on the seat with his ankle tucked under him. His smile was so big Random thought you could have deposited your mail in it.

"Look here," he said. "The real strawberry hill is like this." He put his hands together out in front of him like he was going to do a slap dive into a swimming pool. Random flinched a little, but all Codbill did was move them apart slowly, making two soft curves, like the mounds on the top of a fat strawberry.

"*That* ain't the strawberry. Nossir." His smile got personal. "The strawberry was *on* that. 'Bout that big." He put the tips of his first finger and thumb together. Random thought he was probably trying to make a circle, but it was more like a bird's egg because Codbill's thumb was so fat he could hardly bend it. "Red, and even had the little spots on it like the seeds on a real one. Said it was a birthmark."

Random tried not to look as blank as he felt, but when Codbill's eyes went from looking at the strawberry back to him they grew thin and the smile shrank from his face.

"Come on," Codbill said, reaching behind himself to open the door. He spun around and hopped out. "Let's go find *you* something to remember." Just before he closed the door Codbill looked at Random in a way that made him feel like he was in the wrong place. It was more than being at the fair, or hanging around in the doorway at Truffer's party. He felt briefly like it was a mistake to be on the planet. The whole dumb planet, he thought.

Random grabbed the door handle and it came off in his hand. He said *Shit* like he was spitting on the city dump, and would've thrown the handle through the windshield except when he brought his arm up the handle bumped the ceiling and whanged off into the back seat. He hurt his finger, too, cussed again, and brought his fist down on the dashboard.

"Ain't no future in this," he heard himself yell, and then it grew suddenly quiet and he saw Codbill through the window waving him to come on. Codbill was standing in front of a Pontiac the hanging lights were gleaming off of, so it looked as if everything in the fair had exploded and all the pieces had floated down on him.

Random slid across the seat and got out the driver's door. He jogged and caught up with Codbill at the gate. "Here," Codbill said, shoving a ticket in his hand. "It's on me."

<hr />

They went past the big pavilions that had exhibits and farm shows, down to the midway where the game stalls started. It was the second week of the fair, so the smells of the animals and grease and people weren't any different from the air they breathed.

At the rifle range Random shot twenty straight bull's-eyes on the turning bear, kept him facing frontwards the whole time, twitching and roaring. After the twentieth shot the light in the circle on his belly went out and he leaned half over and quit moving. The last roar died down to a groan like a record slowing up with the needle still on it.

Random straightened up and fitted the rifle back in its holder. The old man behind the counter handed him a big black-and-white panda.

Codbill pulled his arm and they went past three or four more stalls. Random thought they were moving aimlessly until he noticed Codbill had been touching his arm, the one holding the panda, leaning a little into him, or seeming to get in the way occasionally as they walked. When they started down a sideshoot off the main midway, he realized Codbill had been guiding him.

It was darker and there was a mixture of different kinds of thudding music all around. Just ahead of him he saw a series of four bare wood platforms strung out on each side, each one in front of a curtain with a sign tacked to it.

"What chew been waiting for all your life," Codbill said. It seemed to Random that he hummed it. "What chew been dreaming *of.*" Random heard him say the last word as if it were the most important one in the sentence, as sometimes in the driving of a nail the last lick is the hardest. He stopped beside the first platform.

Random had heard of Freak Alley. Some of the guys who'd been to the fair last year had made it sound pretty gross to him, even though they'd probably invented a lot of it, as he suspected they did in the locker room when they talked about girls. It was the same people, too, he'd noticed. It can't be all that weird, he figured.

He shifted the panda into his left arm and leaned his head on it for a second, feeling the cool material against his cheek, thinking about going back to the main midway to throw soggy baseballs at the grinning cats. As he turned he saw the sign for the Fat Lady.

"Un-unh," Codbill said from behind him, and gave him another push. "Not for us. You can see ten of her at the next football game. Some mothers, even."

He guided Random past the sign showing a man eating swords and fire. The next one was painted to look like a poker card, with MADAME written across its top and bottom. Random didn't get a chance to see the picture though, because Codbill cut them across to the other side of the alley. They stopped in front of the last platform.

The sign said HALF MAN HALF WOMAN and the picture showed a woman with a beard. She looked to Random about as big as the Fat Lady's picture, but with muscles instead of fat. Her head was almost square, and her hair wasn't very long. She looked as if someone had measured it and then cut it the same all around. Random guessed it could've been a wig, and the beard fake, too. He shifted his panda so he was hugging it with both arms.

As his mind began to drift back toward the main midway again, Codbill said, "What it's all about," sounding to Random like he'd discovered America, or the New Hebrides, which Random had read about in social studies last week and mispronounced. He looked over at Codbill.

Codbill's knees were bent and his round body was rocking a little. His words came out in a rhythm like they were going back and forth, too.

"Yes. Yes. It's the army and the navy and the air force one on one. The last roundup ervy time." When he turned his smile toward Random, Random had the impression that the grease from his hair had gotten on it; his expression became blank. Random thought, he's staring at me but not really looking at me, or anything.

"Counts," Codbill said. "Counts." His body got still. "Them dumb mohair bitches don't know their twats from a Coke bottle. Ought to have their next party here."

Random took the big explosion that came out of his mouth to be a laugh, because the next thing he said sounded happy, and his little black eyes seemed to start seeing again.

"All they'd have to do is line up here and go through the tent and kiss old Misterwoman in there. Haw. Boys could do it, girls could do it, no need to spin no bottle or fight over who gets who." He wound down a little, reminding Random of the bear— he even seemed to get shorter for a second. He took a deep breath and when he let it out the word *shit* came out with it, softer than Random usually heard it.

"But they won't let us in there," Random said. He pointed to a sign tacked on the flap of the canvas they used for a door: No One Under 21 Years of Age Admitted to This Attraction.

"They don't care," Codbill said. "And it don't matter anyhow. We're not going in that way."

He walked to the end of the tent. When he disappeared around the side, Random followed him, flipping the panda over longways under his right arm. When he turned the corner Codbill was lying on the ground holding the bottom edge of the tent up and looking under it. His other arm was motioning Random to crawl under.

Random knelt and looked in; he couldn't see anything but feet and cigarette butts and bright lights up at the stage end. He flattened out and slid under, pulling the panda in after him.

"Move," Codbill hissed, and pushed Random with his foot. Random edged over some more and Codbill rolled into the tent. They lay still a minute and then snuck to the back, not exactly crawling Random thought, but more like commandoes hunched over close to the dirt.

They sat down on the end of the next to last bench. Random didn't look at the smelly man Codbill pushed him up against because he was too busy watching the person on the stage.

It looked to Random as if it weighed three hundred pounds, easily. He thought it looked something like the picture outside, but nothing at all like it, too. Its hair was cut even all around, straight across the forehead, and the head was square. Random thought of Prince Valiant, but this had a mustache instead of the beard he'd seen on the poster outside. What impressed him most, however, was the color. The person's skin resembled chalk with pink paint on it. Its cheeks and nose and chin had splotches that looked as if they'd been red once but needed touching up.

And the sweat. Even from where they were—which wasn't all that far back, maybe twenty-five or thirty feet—he could see the sweat rolling down the face and off the shoulders and into the gap between the breasts. There was a string of bulbs hung up behind a board above the stage, and the light from them gleamed on the trickles of sweat.

The Half Man Half Woman was sitting on a tall stool and wore a plain blue skirt and a sleeveless T-shirt like a basketball jersey—yellow with big red flowers blooming over the breasts. It was tight, accentuating the rolls of fat underneath. The more Random watched, the more trouble he had telling the waves of fat from the breasts.

On the stage the skinny man in a brown sweater talking about how the person was both a man and a woman was getting heated up by the time Random began to hear what he was saying. Codbill poked the panda with his elbow and said, "We got in here at the best time. Watch this."

"If you're still not convinced," the skinny man said, lighting a cigarette, "if it hadn't been enough to hear a man's voice come out of a long-haired person, or see a mustache and these"—he pointed with his cigarette hand at the swells under the top of the sleeveless shirt—"then you got one more think coming."

The manwoman got down off the stool, leaning a hand on the skinny person's shoulder. The skinny man faked as if he were going to break under the load, or maybe he was for all Random knew; the other people in the tent laughed. From the noise Random realized how quiet it had been. He looked around and figured there were eighteen or twenty men sitting on the benches.

The manwoman stood by the stool. The skirt stopped above the knees; the legs looked to Random like she could play fullback for the Washington Redskins, except, he noticed at the same instant, they didn't have any hair.

It grew quiet again. The skinny man had gone off the stage and came back pushing two crudely fashioned, L-shaped wooden stools like the ones Random's grandfather used for gout, only not padded. He set them about three or four feet apart, facing the woman.

Then somebody threw him another stool from offstage, just like the one the manwoman had been sitting on, but half as tall. He positioned that one behind her and she sat down on it.

The skinny man mashed out his cigarette, twisting his shoe on it. He came around and hoisted each of the manwoman's legs up on the other stools so she was sitting there V-eed out at the audience. Random started to sweat and tingle, and pressed the panda against himself.

"Now," the skinny man said again, "you get the piece of resistance, the whole shooting match. If you go out of here after this without believing what you've seen, it's not my fault."

He backed off to the side of the stage and pointed to the manwoman, who was swaying back and forth a little, hitching up her skirt. Somebody offstage put on a scratchy record of a march, reminding Random of a July Fourth parade.

The man yelled, "First the morphydite will show you her male organ, and after that he will show you his female one."

To Random's astonishment, that's what the manwoman did. It got its skirt all the way up and spread its legs out wider on the stools. Then it put its hands down in its crotch and pulled the fat apart.

First he saw a pecker, small but unmistakable, and then he, or she—he couldn't say to himself exactly which was right—moved that aside and with her fingers pried apart two folds of skin, revealing a deep crease right where Random knew it was supposed to be, colored a faded red like the spots on her face. It seemed to Random almost not to have happened it stopped so abruptly, but he saw it, or thought he did, as substantial as a bullwhip cracking through the air.

He felt dried up and desperate. Reflexively his right hand went to his crotch. He cupped his sex as if to stop it from shriveling up and disappearing inside him. If I don't get out of here now, he thought, there won't be any help for me anymore.

He shoved the panda away. It fell half over and then leaned against the bench in front of him. He stomped it with his right foot and it jammed under the wood.

He stood up and stared down at Codbill, who was laughing fit to kill, head back and roaring. He had his right leg up on the bench in front.

"What's so funny?" Random said.

He laughed some more, bending his head over forward so Random saw the part in his greasy hair again. Random heard himself yell, "Wildroot Cream Oil," at Codbill and then, in a tone whose meanness wasn't familiar, "You fat little sonofabitch, lemme out."

He pushed against Codbill's leg, but Codbill didn't move it, just made his mouth into a round grin that seemed to swell toward Random as if to swallow him. Random kicked up with his right foot. Codbill's body spun around sideways and Random squeezed by.

He went through the open tent flap just like he was supposed to be there. Out in the alley the air was filling up with smoke from the cigarettes the men had lit who'd just seen what he had. He wanted to take a deep breath, but couldn't.

There didn't seem much sense in running, either, although he wanted to. All there seemed to be was more fair, and Codbill's car, or somebody else's, in the parking lot, and anonymous parties all over the place with lights for people to hang colored paper on so you couldn't tell who was who, or doing what, much less yourself, and someone standing angrily over someone else, yelling, and people ready to march downstairs and crack their whips to make you feel like whatever it was was all wrong anyway.

"Shit," he said, and brought his leg up and then back down, hard, so his heel stuck in the ground.

"Don't worry about it. It's no big deal." Codbill had come up beside him. For an instant, Random saw two Codbills, the person and a funny copy of the person, at once, like a photograph next to a negative.

"Hell," Random said to both of them. "What do *you* know? That's not just some freak in there for you to laugh at. Or somebody playing a cheap trick too deep to figure out."

"What is it, then?" The question still seemed to come from the two forms standing beside Random, so he turned and looked more closely, finally distinguishing Codbill from the panda Codbill was holding.

"It's . . . shit . . . it's everything. It's you. Or Edith." His arm shot out, his forefinger pointing rigidly. "It's your goddamned doll." He heard the perplexity and anger begin to drain from his voice. "I don't know what it is."

Codbill stared at him a moment. "You forgot your prize," he said, holding the black-and-white animal out toward Random. He didn't laugh or sneer, as Random half expected him to, so Random had no excuse to hit him, which he felt like doing. Codbill just said it.

Random looked at him. "You keep it," he said. The levelness of his voice surprised him, as if there were a weight on it keeping it from rising, or he didn't have anything to complain about anymore.

"Or you can give it to your mother," he said. "If you have a mother." He reached out and poked Codbill on the arm with his fist, not hard, and then messed his hair up by rubbing his hand over it a couple of times. Random could feel Codbill trying to keep his head from moving.

He left Codbill standing there, grinning blankly. It wasn't altogether different from how Random felt walking through the smells of cotton candy and animals and cigar smoke and sweat, rubbing his fingers against the inside of his hand, not even wondering what to do next.

HOMESPUN

Now that we know what to say to each other, my brother and I walk under the railroad trestles stacked three-high by the canal. A famous postcard shows a steam engine on each of the trestles at the same time, like a triple-decker sandwich. Nobody I know has ever seen it in real life.

"I can't throw smoke anymore," my brother says. "A cunny-thumb, reduced to junk."

He tosses an oyster shell onto one of the mounds of pulverized oyster shells stretching beside us along the street.

I tell him I keep dreaming I have to go back to school. "Four men in black robes and masks kidnap me in a Rolls-Royce. I see our father unlocking the front door of our house, but I just sit there. I don't even call out to him."

Under the pretense of scratching my beard I glance at my brother. He's studying another shell he's picked up. I reach over and pat his stomach. "You could pitch with that."

"Only forty-five," he says, "and you develop a sense of humor." He smiles vacantly at the shell. "The thing I throw best anymore is the morning paper onto porches when my son oversleeps."

I can't tell if he's going to say anything else. We walk a minute or so in silence, the sound of our soft-soled shoes on the asphalt further muted by the humidity. When he doesn't speak, I tell him more of my dream.

"They drive me through the dark, and then leave me in the car in the middle of a shopping mall, staring through the window at a delicatessen." I crunch something under my shoe, probably another shell. "I can't see why I'm dreaming about going back to school. I thought I graduated enough once."

My brother throws another shell at a trestle girder, sidearm, and misses. The shell skips twice on the bottle-green canal water.

"He's such a pseudoturd," he says. "I love his ass, but hell, I'll be glad when he just comes to visit once a year. With his wife, or something."

I watch the dimple the shell left close on top of the water. I decide I'd just as well finish the dream.

"I can't figure the Rolls-Royce, either. And the delicatessen's empty, no meat, no cheese, nothing, not even those curled-up sausages hanging from the ceiling. People pass me by like I'm not there. I just look at nothing through two panes of glass, the car's and the deli's."

By this time my brother has sat down on the projecting base of another girder. I stop, put my hands in my pants pockets, stare at the canal. Fourteenth Street is only a half block away and I notice the noise of a car approaching the bridge to Mayo Island.

My brother's staring in front of him at his forearms. They're hefty, the skin stretched tightly under the blond hairs so it looks like the insides are pressing to get out. Not muscled, but full, solid. He weighs 185, about twenty pounds more than he should.

He looks at me. "We never had this conversation, you understand. I could wave at all this—those dumb shells, patsy train tracks, the puke they use for water—and it would disappear. But that sumbitchin son of mine won't. It looks like he's not even going to get into college. Only applied to one, and he hasn't got a prayer with it. They put him on a waiting list, and we all know what that means."

"Which one?" I ask him.

"The one I went to. Where he was born." His right hand lifts slightly off his knee, hesitates. Then slides down his calf and hangs limply there, like it's broken.

I pinch the front of my shirt between my thumbs and fingers and pull it away from my chest. Shake it a little, the closest thing to a breeze. I start to say something about who invented July but change my mind. My brother has leaned his head against the girder and is holding the base with his hand.

"Come here," he says. "I swear there's a train coming."

I go over and press my ear to the warm metal, and clasp it in both hands. "I don't hear anything."

"Shit. You never do." He gets up and brushes off the seat of his pants. "Come on, let's walk off a couple blocks so we can watch the sucker go by."

So we walk the rest of the way to Fourteenth and cut a couple blocks to the right, up to Cary. We stop in the doorway recess of the abandoned building where our father had his hardware company offices and warehouse when we were little.

Across the street an old woman spinning on a spinning wheel at the top of some steps is painted on the side of a building. Resembles one of my grandmothers. It's an advertisement for Homespun canned fruits and vegetables. Looks odd painted on bricks.

Sure enough, a train comes. Passes on the middle trestle about forty-five miles an hour, I figure, right fast for being so close to the yards. I start to count the cars, but decide it's too hot even for that.

"Should have been a train robber," my brother says. "Could have had this one easy as ice cream."

He crouches down as if he's an umpire behind the plate, makes a motion like he's hefting his chest protector into place, and watches the train. It turns out to be fairly short and when its caboose has clicked out of sight past a warehouse he whips his body sideways to the right, pumps his arm in and out by his side, like a drive shaft on a steam engine, and hollers "stree-yike." Then he stands up, smiling. "Love to call trains," he says.

"Yeah," I say. "Hard work." I point to the Homespun sign.

"Between you and that old lady up there this could be a helluva neighborhood."

"Him, too," he says. "He could be coordinator of ambition."

I look down from the Homespun ad and see my brother pointing at a rag man—that's what we call them, anyhow—dragging his cart like a rickshaw down Fourteenth Street toward the bridge. His cart's not filled with rags but with bundles of scrap paper, which he hauls to the paper company on Mayo Island and sells for a penny a pound. Least that's what they used to pay.

"What's he doing down here on Sunday?" my brother says. "Paper company's closed."

"I don't know," I say. "Maybe he's going to spend the night by the scales."

He's a skinny, coal-black man with a bald head. Though his body's bent almost double pulling the loaded cart, his head's cocked up so he's looking down the street. If he stood up straight he'd be watching the sky.

"Adam's apple and Adam's curse," my brother says.

The old man passes us and we watch him get nearly under the trestles. His white shirt is stuck to his back so tight you can see the color of his skin through it, and the sole of one of his shoes has worn loose so it flaps when he walks.

He stops at the middle of the bridge and lets the cart down. Stands there for a minute, looking over the bridge rail at the river, the place where I thought his neck was broken working like a hinge. Then he picks the cart up and trudges on. Disappears finally as the bridge bends down toward the island.

"You want a good job," my brother says, "you got to get a good education. Like the ad says."

"Sure," I say. "Tell it to the man who makes Bag Balm."

"Hunh?" he says.

"Never mind," I say, and then get an inspiration. "Tell it to Billy Martin."

"Tell what to Billy Martin?" he says.

"And you tell me I never listen." I look over his shoulder at the empty bridge. A sea gull has settled on one of the concrete stumps that separates the sections of rail from each other. It shifts its feet until it's inched all the way around in a circle.

"Look," I say, my eyes flicking back so I'm looking at his sun-burned face. "Don't worry so much. Let the boy find his own life."

"Happy to," he says, staring me in the eye. "Only tell me how I teach him to start looking."

"He *is* looking," I say.

"And how the fuck do you know that?" he asks me. He stretches his arm up and leans on the glassed part of the front door of the building, an old trick he uses to make himself seem taller than me.

I'm ready to laugh at him for getting so official but don't because the door swings in under the pressure of his hand. He almost falls down, then laughs himself.

"Come into my sanctum," he says. He pushes the door back and forth a couple times. "Sucker won't creak. So much for old-time radio." He smiles. "What's really odd is that it's unlocked."

We go into the main area that used to be for reception and information, and a general hallway connecting everything else—the two retail departments on the right, offices to the left, and straight ahead, beyond the turning at the water cooler, the main access to the warehouse.

I walk over and stand behind the big oak sales counter still moored to the floor. The sun hitting the layered dust on the plate glass windows across the front makes an opaque glare you can't look at, much less see through. The oak file drawers have been torn to pieces and strewn over the floor.

"Nothing here," I say, running my finger through the quarter inch of dust on the counter. "Same nothing that's been here for twenty-five years."

My brother's walked halfway to the musty darkness at the back. I remember an open light bulb used to hang from the ceiling above the water cooler, but it always seemed scary anyway.

"Maybe so," he says, "maybe not," and disappears around the corner.

I follow him, the floorboards creaking under my feet no different from what they'd done when I was twelve. I pass through the dark turning in the hall, notice the doors to the toilets are gone, likewise those to the warehouse, and step into what used to be the assembly area for local orders.

It runs right to left a total of a hundred feet or so, with huge sliding iron doors at each end that open onto railroad sidings. The one on the left, closer to me, looks so rusty it'd take a power winch to pull it open.

A few flattened cartons are scattered around, but the room is empty otherwise, cavernous, the air thick with disuse. It feels like if you spoke too loudly or moved too quickly a membranous stickiness would rise up and envelop your body. It's almost pitch-dark down at the far end by the freight elevator.

My brother's nowhere to be seen.

I go over and stand on the scales mounted in the floor. I'm surprised to find them still there, even though my weight doesn't register. A few of the slotted disk weights are stacked at the back, rusted, too.

I lean on the upright arm of the scales facing the open end of the metal chute spiraling down from the upper floors. When we were children we used to spend some Saturday mornings sliding down it on cardboard squares.

"That's got to be it," I say softly. "He's gone upstairs to slide down the chute."

I wait three or four minutes, expecting his cannonballed body to come spurting around the last curve in the chute, but instead hear his footsteps creaking the floorboards above my head. He crosses the floor and descends the stairs.

He stops in the warehouse doorway, a strange empty look on his face, his mouth working like it can't find the expression it wants.

"Couldn't do it," he says. "Walked all the way to the top floor and just stood there at the beginning of the thing and couldn't sit down and push off." He shakes his head and some of the distortion on his face eases. "Like my legs were locked all the way up into my shoulders, only they weren't." He looks at the floor. "Goddamnit, they weren't."

He cries out the last part and hits the doorjamb. Leaves his fist against the wood and turns it slightly, back and forth, as if trying to auger it in.

He stares at his fist a few seconds. Then I see his eyes drift over to the plate glass window of what used to be the shipping clerk's office. Slowly his face comes back to normal and he quits twisting himself into the wood.

"Look at this," he says. "Would you come here and look at this?" He walks over and pushes open the door to the clerk's office. The scales shake heavily as I step off of them. I go and stand behind him in the doorway and look over his shoulder.

The office is immaculate, almost Spartan, like a cell in a monastery. One cot, perfectly made up, along one of the walls, a small table with one drawer beside the cot, a lamp on the table, a straight-back chair, a round-topped, half-sized steamer trunk beside the other wall. The room clearly is dusted and swept regularly. It almost smells clean.

"Holy of holies," my brother says. "Wonder who this little rent-free retreat belongs to."

"No telling," I say. "But suddenly I don't feel very good about being here. Let's go." I take my hand off the doorjamb and start to walk toward the door back into the main offices.

"Yeah," he says. "Me, too. But we ought to leave a calling card or something."

He steps back from the doorway and looks around the floor. Near the scales is a small scattering of excelsior, so dusty it's the color of a battleship. He picks up three or four strands and, stooping down, arranges them on the floor just inside the threshold of the furnished room.

"Answer one mystery with another," he says. He stands up

and turns toward me. He sweeps his hand in an arc and bows a little, like he's a courtier with a plumed hat from some old play. "This place sent us to college. 'The store' he called it."

He lets his hand fall to his side. "Shit," he says. "I wouldn't be surprised if he walked in the front door and came back here and sat on the cot and took his shoes off. You remember how he used to unlace his shoes? One leg crossed on the other knee so he wouldn't have to bend over."

I nod at him. "I saw a man do cat's cradle with string once, up North somewhere. It reminded me of Daddy's undoing his laces. I half-expected music to come out of them sometimes."

We stare at each other for a second or two. Then he comes past me and goes on toward the front of the building, touching my shoulder as he passes.

I look down at the three or four strands of excelsior tangled at the entrance to the strange room, then turn and follow him.

Outside, clouds have gathered over the river. It's cooler, or the air feels like it's thinned, which is funny for July just before a storm.

My brother's standing across the street under the Homespun sign, his hands in his pockets. He points at the clouds and I nod. Some thunder rumbles upriver toward Goochland.

"Let's go get the car," he says, his words soft and clear from across the street.

"Okay," I say. I reach down and check to see the door's closed tightly against the weather. When I look up I see the rag man cresting the bridge, on his way back.

EASY

DUPO

Herman and me and Sister Vermean were standing on the beach watching the Atlantic Ocean. Herman lives on the island all the time, and Sister Vermean spends a lot of time down here visiting her uncle, but it's my first trip. The uncle is my uncle, too, which makes Sister Vermean some sort of cousin. The way my family gets shuffled around during Christmas gets pretty complicated sometimes.

The weather was normal for December, or so Sister Vermean said—clear but gray. The sand and water and sky blended into each other at their lines, but you could still tell which was which.

We were looking out over the water from a log, big and slanted along the edges like a ceiling timber; the surf would roll up toward us and thin out just short of our toes. Herman called it "surveying the domain." Which we'd been doing every late afternoon during our vacation, but not usually perched on anything.

"What's that?" Herman says.

"Haanh?" Sister Vermean says. She drags the sound out like it's taffy she's pulling off her teeth.

"That." Herman points out toward England, which is nowhere as far as I'm concerned. I don't see anything.

"Oh yeah." Sister Vermean lays one hand on my shoulder to turn me, and points more at a place than Herman had. I see three objects way the hell out there, smaller than flies almost.

"Probably boats," I say.

"Maybe they've just landed," Herman says. "Maybe we'll be the first to see the creatures."

"Sure, Herman," I say. Sister Vermean and I look at each other and then at the surf, which is about to run up over the log. We jump off backwards and watch Herman's sneakers get soaked. He doesn't even look down, just stands there leaning on his dead palmetto frond, watching his UFOs out on the Atlantic.

Sister Vermean and I kill some time checking out a load of shells at the last high-tide line. Not a whole shell in the bunch, just fragments, like always.

When we walk back down to Herman the objects have gotten closer. They look to me like handlebar mustaches spread out across big floating things like the wooden tubs in *Swiss Family Robinson*.

"Three Rollie Fingers," Herman says, like he'd been inside my head.

"Who's Three Rawlee Fingers?" Sister Vermean wants to know.

I open my mouth but it's too long to explain, so after a minute I just say, "A fireman."

"Lifesaver," Herman says, "summoned from the bullpen." He makes a shelf over his eyes with his hand and cranes his neck. "Low and outside."

"You guys," Sister Vermean says. "I wonder how I find time." She's turned her head down the beach so I can't see her face, but I figure she's rolling her eyes up like she does. Next thing, she'll tell one of us we've been drinking too much.

"You drink too much, George," she says.

Herman's let his hand down by now, and is sweeping the water with his palm frond. "He doesn't drink George," he says. "Not too often."

Sister Vermean takes a dozen steps down the beach, sort of skidding her heels. She stops and points up at the clouds beginning to color some from the low sun behind us.

"Jeez," she says. "Look at that. Magenta, peach, flame, naples yellow." Her finger moves from spot to spot like she's ticking items off a shopping list.

Herman's voice comes down the breeze toward us. "Here we are in the presence of extraterrestrial beings moving in, and you talk about the stupid sunset."

"Haanh?" Sister Vermean says and looks over her shoulder at me. She waves at Herman to come on and walk with us, but he turns his head back toward his objects on the ocean. The surf slops all the way over the log and his sneakers, thinning out about ten feet behind him.

By this time Sister Vermean and I are close enough to the end of the spit to see a figure hunched in the dune grass by a junked windsurfer. When it rises up it seems smaller than when it was sitting down. It jerks a step or two toward us, looking tilted.

"Hey, DuPo," Sister Vermean calls.

The creature stops and leans its head sideways like it's listening to its shoulder. The leg on the same side it's listening to looks jammed up into the middle of its body. I think for a minute there's a rubber band stretched from his ear to his knee, trying to twist him out of shape, and he's pulling just as hard against it. Looks tight as a bow too stiff to string.

His free arm goes whipping straight up in the air like a flag on a pole. He smiles at us, or probably at Sister Vermean.

"Who's that?" I ask her.

"DuPo," she says, like I hadn't already heard that much. "From over Harbor Town. Lives on the beach mostly. Scavenges and stuff." She goes over to him. "How about that sunset?" she says.

"Yeah, yeah, yeah," DuPo says, his head nodding with each word. "O. Kay. A."

We stand there a minute. DuPo looks at the sand, his eyes skittering back and forth like sandpipers chasing the surf. Sister Vermean stares at the clouds, which sooner or later she will tell us are getting really intense.

I hear Herman's voice and turn around. He's running down

the beach toward us, holding his palmetto frond in both hands above his head like a soldier carrying his rifle in deep water. He's yelling something I can't understand. Then he switches to cantering like a horse, bowing his head and raising it as he moves.

I feel DuPo brush against me as he lurches by. His arm on the long side is halfway up in Herman's direction.

Herman is yelling in the middle of a canter when he sees DuPo. His mouth and his body stop all at once. As quickly as he was moving across the sand he is standing dead still on it. Silent as a dune. He lets the brown frond come down slowly in his right hand until it hangs by his leg.

"DuPo." He says it like you would say *trout* or *flounder* to somebody who'd never seen them before.

DuPo nods. His free arm springs out by his side at the ocean. Sister Vermean and Herman and I look out like one person where he's pointing.

I've forgotten about the objects. They seem close enough to touch now, looming up on us like they really are going to land and let off some kind of strange cargo. They're not really that close, of course, probably still a mile off shore, but for a second it's weird, like in the movies when a scene is up real close and then shoots off far away again, real quick.

"Shrippodes, shrippodes, shrippodes," DuPo says, a word for each boat. His arm goes up and down like a signal at a railroad crossing. He smiles.

The three shrimp boats have turned so you can see what they are. Their white hulls and cabins are outlined against the darker horizon behind them.

"Their nets are pendulous from the spars," Herman says, like some preacher.

The air around the boats looks vague and gray. Over the cove they're aimed at hang Sister Vermean's colored clouds.

"What are those black things flying all over the ships?" Sister Vermean says.

"Shrimp," Herman says. "Holy shrimp."

"So *they're* the holy shrimp," I say. If Herman's not going to quit, then neither am I. I expect Sister Vermean to say *Haanh?* but she tightens up her eyebrows and looks first at DuPo, then back out at the shrimp boats.

"I didn't know shrimp fly."

"Sure." Herman starts walking back down toward the surf. Sister Vermean follows like she wants us to think she's on a leash. Me and DuPo sort of straggle after.

"These particular ones, though, are special. They only appear during Christmas."

"But that's two days away," Sister Vermean says.

"The Christmas *season*," Herman says. So far he hasn't looked at Sister Vermean, probably because he thinks he's got her hooked and doesn't have to make her feel really dumb to keep things going. He drags the palmetto frond behind him. It makes grooves through his shallow footprints.

We get down to where the edge of the surf thins out again. "The holy shrimp nested in the boats' nets last night." Herman sweeps his frond out at arm's length and then lets it hang by his side. "This morning the shrimp woke up and flew into the air, carrying the nets up like sails." He looks down at a wave breaking. "Whistling. Yes. The shrimp whistle while they fly."

"I don't hear anything," Sister Vermean says.

"Not now you don't, because they only whistle going *out* to sea. It's their way of blessing the beginning of the trip."

Sister Vermean looks up at Herman when he says *blessing,* or I think she does, but she doesn't say anything.

"The shrimp," Herman says, turning sideways to the boats and looking Sister Vermean in the eye like DuPo and I weren't there, "these holy shrimp guarantee a great catch to the boats they fly with. Only happens once a year, around here at least." Pointing out at the boats with his frond but still looking at Sister Vermean, he says, "See how much lower they are in the water now than they usually are."

This time Sister Vermean says *Haanh* and grabs herself on the waist, one hand at each side. "I don't know where you're *from*," she says, "but I think I'm beginning to know what you eat."

The boats have begun to go past us, so we are looking at them from behind, partly, at an angle. The sky over the inlet has turned a deep rich color like one of those French wines when you pour it out of its dark bottle into a glass.

Herman looks up there like he's trying to find something to say, but before he can we all see DuPo kneeling at the edge of the surf. He's putting handfuls of wet sand around Herman's feet. He builds a little donut around each sneaker, and then starts filling in the holes, which makes upside-down cones on Herman's feet.

DuPo pats each one down real good and stands up. He lifts the palmetto frond out of Herman's hand and takes a couple steps backward. His stiff side all of a sudden twitches from bottom to top like a piece of cooked spaghetti wiggling off a fork.

"Where's your Mama, DuPo?" Herman says, like he's brushing away a fly.

"Whesho Ma Ma?" DuPo says back. It's not an echo because you can tell DuPo is really asking a question.

"I know where mine is," Sister Vermean says.

DuPo holds the palmetto frond with both hands by its broom part and points the stiff end at Sister Vermean.

"Sho Ma Ma," he says.

"Hanging stupidass colored balls on a stupidass dumb tree. Pretending how to be happy." Sister Vermean's voice could open a safe without the combination. "Talking some phony goodtime trash on the rocks to some stupidjackass . . . I don't know." Her voice thickens up some, and slows down. "Just as well be on another planet as six hundred miles from here."

"Stupi dass," says DuPo.

"Aanh haanh," says Sister Vermean, and tears the frond out of DuPo's hand, starts yelling and spinning around in circles with it. When she lets it go it flies a little way out and fluffs down into the surf. Sister Vermean loses her balance and falls down.

Nobody says anything for a minute.

Sister Vermean picks herself up and brushes her britches off. The dark cones of sand on Herman's feet look heavy as lead. DuPo's hands are still out where they were when he was holding the frond, like they're frozen. His eyes look all wrinkled and red.

We are all staring at each other.

When I look for the shrimp boats again they're gone. The ocean is empty, and there's nothing in the inlet but the last glow of the clouds reflected in the water.

It's hard for me to tell what the others see, or want. Myself, I wonder if they feel like they've been stuck here by somebody, like I do, without having any say-so about it. I know it isn't where I'd like to be anymore, if it ever was.

EASY

The Celtic Café was a belchy place, the air almost the same color as the Guinness on tap, but every time I walked into it from a bright, sunshiny morning I could still see everything. Didn't need a second for my eyes to get used to the dark. Come through the door and see the tables with their thick glass ashtrays and salt-shakers, the line down the front of the bar where the wood curved up to make a bumper, the faces of whoever was in there. At 10 A.M. there weren't too many, but you could tell who they were, and speak and be friendly, and set your bottom down and have a Knick or a little Knick. And pass the time.

It's not that I come in that often, but this morning my wife had told me she was pregnant, just like that, as she left for work, so I came on down, knowing I could get comfortable and out of the world's way for a while.

I walked in, didn't need to squint or stand in the doorway, and said hello to Will, the bartender.

"Hey, Chance," he said. "What're you drinking?"

I didn't know, so I just eased my parts up onto a stool and looked around.

Everything seemed pretty normal except there were more people than usual at the tables. In fact, the place was almost full. I turned my head toward the bartender and was going to say something about business being good, but what I saw stopped my mouth in mid-open, so to speak.

The rows and rows of bottles that usually sat behind the bar were gone. The shades of green and amber, the pale gins and vodkas, the bright red and yellow labels, gone. And the big mirror, too, with beveled edges and as long as a Pullman car, gone.

In fact, what I'd always thought were shelves had been turned into a sort of stage, very shallow, with room for only a row of chairs that went from one end of the bar to the other. A bunch of old men were sitting in them.

"What's happened to the bottles, Will?" I said. "And the taps. You not going out of business?" I meant the questions to be confidential for the bartender, but my voice came out loud enough for everybody to hear.

There was some murmuring, none of which I could make out, and then the guy down a couple stools told me it was the contest.

"What contest?" I said.

"Bartender of the year. Have it at different bars each time. This year's the Celtic's turn."

My mouth was still half open and I wasn't really looking at anything, staring at the row of old men without seeing them. Probably looked as dumb as I felt.

Will came up to my end of the bar and leaned on it, turning so that while he talked to me he could watch the men in the chairs.

I made myself look at them. There were a dozen, divided in half by a twelve-inch space between chairs after the first six. The group nearer me wore blue seersucker suits, white shirts with rumpled, unbuttoned collars, and dark ties loosely hanging down past the third button. The other six wore gray, collarless pajamas that looked like they'd been slept in for months.

It wouldn't be altogether true to say they looked alike, but their faces were almost the same, if that makes any sense. Sort of square-shaped, with a broad forehead, slightly large nose, full mouth. The eyes were alert enough but they were empty from looking too long at something, as if they were afraid they might see whatever it was they were seeing. They all had gray bushy hair and a couple days' thick stubble the same color, like the Perfect Circle Piston Ring guy. Tough but Oh so gentle. They just sat there, staring, half-slumped down in the straight chairs.

They reminded me of the actors on TV that play disgruntled, second-rate cops who've never gotten promoted enough. The kind with potbellies and whiskey breath who botch up their own suicides, maybe because the hose from the exhaust pipe to the car window has a big hole in it, or they can't get the garage door shut all the way. So they come to work the next morning with their front shirttail a little more out, and rub their cheek.

Only these guys were bartenders, or so I was told.

"Whadya think?" Will said.

"About what?" I said.

"Them." He made a sweeping half circle with his right hand. "Good bunch, hunh? Lot bettern last year, I can tell you that."

"You can say that again," the man down the bar from me said. "You remember the guy who won last year? That junkie or something. Had a pinhead. Didn't know a martini from a slot machine."

"Last year was a mistake. A total mistake," Will said. "Not worth the shot to blow it away."

"You can say that again," the man said.

"But this year's different," Will said, sweeping his hand toward the old men again and turning back to me, grinning. "Whadya think?"

"How old are they?" I couldn't think of anything else to say. Then I did. "Gimme a Knick."

"Run from about twenty-five to fifty-five, I'd guess," Will said. "That one third from the other end's probably the oldest. Spender, from Somerville. You don't have no trouble picking the youngest, you can tell him by the crewcut and the smirk."

The noise level in the place had risen so I couldn't hear Will's answer too well, or didn't want to. I looked at the men again, propped in the chairs under the bank of hard white lights, and saw what I'd already seen. Old men, lookalikes, blankly terrified. Shit, one of them looked something like my father.

"Gimme a Knick," I said again, but Will had gone down to

the guys in pajamas and was tying one of 'em's shoe. They all had on fancy brown wingtips.

Will stood up and said something to the men. None of them looked at him but they seemed to be listening. A couple of the ones in suits took combs out of their coat pockets and began combing their hair. One of the guys in pajamas stood up and started to make a humming noise with his mouth open. A few stretched.

Will came back up to my end of the bar.

"What happens next?" I said.

"Testimonials. They tell why they think they ought to win the award."

"What's the award?"

"Nobody knows each year until it's given. Except the prize committee, but after they meet and decide on it they're isolated until the winner's picked. So they don't leak anything." Will mined his left nostril delicately with a little finger.

"Isolated?" I said.

"Yeah. Like a jury. Except it's another word. Secrested, or something."

"Sequestered," I said.

He wiped his finger on his apron. "Whatever," he said. "Couple years back the award was a year off with pay. Each bar chipped in each month. Poor guy went nuts after a while with nothing to do. Tried to hang himself."

All but one of the men had settled back down into their chairs, like they were before, like someone had told each one of them their position and their bodies remembered. Slumped, empty-looking, like dummies. The other one had rolled up his pajama leg and was rubbing his shin, up and down over and over again, like he was shining it.

"Don't they have to mix a drink, or something, to show what they can do?" I said.

Will looked at me funny. "Naw. They're bartenders, ain't they? Everybody knows they can make a drink. After the testimonials they sing a song of their choice." He looked back at the men and smiled, like he was a trainer who'd gotten them in shape for this. "You want anything?" he said, turning back to me.

"A Knick," I said, but then for some reason changed my mind. "No, nothing."

The last one had quit rubbing his shin and sat down. Seeing them again all in a row like that, little beads of sweat glistening on their foreheads under the lights, their mouths drawn into thin lines, did something to me.

I don't know how to say exactly what.

The stubble on their faces was longer, it was like I could actually see it growing—only it wasn't going to get softer or grow into a nice full beard, it was going to stay stubble, gritty and rasping and stiff.

I had a strange thought. Nobody is going to harvest it. The stubble, I mean. The stubble is never going to be harvested.

I got down slowly off my stool and backed toward the door. Crazy as it sounds, I felt like the goddamn stubble was aimed at me. I fumbled the door open and slipped out into the coarse sunlight.

I turned around and leaned against the big Celtic window. I was still seeing those men lined up before me, stretching down the street, like I had carried them outdoors in my eyes. Then they wavered, a whip lashing in slow motion, and the next thing I knew Easy was standing in front of me. Cars going by, the parking meters shining, people walking past, and Easy popping up out of nowhere.

"You going in?" he said.

"Hunh?" I looked at his black eyepatch, and then into his good eye, which slipped around in the white like a stuffed animal's. "No," I said, "coming out."

"Where you going?" he said.

I opened my mouth automatically but the automatic word didn't come out. So I admitted I didn't know.

"Let's go shine the car then," Easy said, hoisting his low shoulder, and pivoting on his wooden leg.

Easy made whatever living he could waxing cars. He called it "Simonizing" because that was the only wax he'd use. Had no truck with this no-buffing, miracle stuff. People said he lived in East Cambridge, nobody knew exactly where, but it had been enough to give him a name, E. C., which had gotten to be Easy long before I was born.

How he'd gotten banged up and scarred and half-blinded nobody knew either. And whatever he'd retreated from was now so far away even he couldn't remember it, or so it seemed.

This was the first time I'd ever seen him not shining a car, or sitting on one he thought needed it.

"My wife's got it at work," I said.

He finished the pivot, took a couple steps, and stopped. I saw the muscles on one side of his back wiggle under his coat. He stretched and turned his neck as if he were trying to drag the muscles out of a hiding place. I thought the little tote he carried his wax and rags in was going to slip off his rounded shoulder.

"She's pregnant," I said.

Easy whipped back around, throwing his arms out for balance, his short coattails whirling briefly. He walked up to me and gripped one of my arms just above the elbow. I'm five foot eleven, and he came up to my chest, and his hand through my sweater felt small and bony, but at the same time I felt like he could have crushed my arm without trying very hard.

He was smiling at me.

"Don't have much say who your children are," he said. "Have less your parents. Congratulations."

"Thanks," I said. I looked past his face at the front of the Celtic Café and saw the traffic and the street reflected in part of the big window. The sun hit the other part so it glared painfully. I looked down at the sidewalk.

"Where's she work at?" he said.

"Shady Side School," I said. "In the treasurer's office." I started to ask why, but realized before I could get the word out.

"You're not going to walk all that far to shine my car?" I imagined his wrenched little body lurching along on that wooden leg. "Jesus, Easy, that's almost three miles."

"Nook," he said. His unshaven face scrunched up but the smile was still discernible. "Nook. We got all day, hain't we? We'll get some eats at de Trowbitch on the way. C'mon. You got anybody else to cerberate wif?"

Shady Side was nothing for me. I walked almost that far every day to the graduate engineering library, where I was working on my degree. But by the time we got there at about two o'clock I was out of breath and Easy looked like all he'd done was go around the block on a motor scooter.

He ate a roast beef sub at the Trowbridge Spa, smiling at me past the gaps in his teeth, chewing and gumming, and washed it down with a beer.

The rest of the way we didn't talk much. When I asked him why he didn't go through the university grounds instead of taking the long way round on the streets, he shot his short arm up into the air and said something about happenings, or happiness, I couldn't tell, and started walking a little faster, his tote bumping against his hip.

He spotted the car before I did, and headed for it. I stopped and watched him walk around it, giving it the once-over like he was thinking of buying it and not just giving it a shine job. It was a '53 Ford my wife's father had given her, two-door hardtop, salmon and white. Easy loved to work on it because the pink part took the wax like dry wood takes oil.

He did a little jig with one hand against a fender for balance and hopped up on the hood. The guy was so full of himself you'd have thought he was a goddamn pixie or something, light-footed and graceful as a dancer; it almost made you forget his greasy clothes, and the terrible distortions of his body.

I crossed the street and leaned on the car beside him. His fingerprints where he'd balanced himself showed clearly on the faded salmon fender.

"I can't afford this, Easy," I said. "You know that. I haven't paid you since last time, and that was when there was still snow in the gutters."

"Yeah, I know," he said. He stretched his neck and examined the roof. "Nemmind that. I got the day, and you looking, so why not? You know what I mean?"

"No," I said, smiling at his curled mouth, feeling a surge of warmth toward him sitting there, small and unattested, just one person being himself. "I never do."

"Comes a time you shine," he said, letting his fingers trail over the wiper blades. "Don't know how to do no bettern that, for myself or nobody. Nook."

He lifted his feet and legs up and spun around on his fanny. Then slid off the other side of the hood onto the sidewalk and started digging into his tote.

I put the tips of my fingers against the dark fingerprints he'd left on the fender, taking away a little of the smudge on my skin. I wiped it on my pants and turned and looked across the street at Shady Side School.

I saw my wife through one of the windows. I waved, but with the sun reflecting in the panes it was hard to tell if she saw me, or was even looking. Come to think of it I wasn't sure it was her, but it didn't seem to matter. I waved some more, harder, and began to smile.

I couldn't figure it out, but right then the faces of the men at the bar popped into my mind. I saw them lined up and tried to imagine how the winner would look when his name was announced, what he'd do when he knew he'd gotten the prize, whatever it was.

I turn and look at Easy through the windows of the Ford. He's working on the right front door, hunched down so I can't see his body, just his face above the lower edge of the window. His tongue pokes out of the corner of his mouth. The ropy muscles in his neck are tight, sticking up slightly. At that moment there seems to be nothing else in the world for him but the spot he's shining.

Then the men standing there in my mind—grizzled and dazed, old as alcohol itself—bow; the line of them, as if they were a chorus of dancing girls who had practiced for months, as if they were all winners, bows in perfect unison.

Nothing else about them changes at all, except maybe for the little flecks of light that catch in the stubble of the one who looks like my father, which is all of them.

I look up at the school again. This time the sun fills the panes of the window. No one could be there, but I wave anyhow. I'm not grinning like an empty mirror any more, just standing in the street, one hand settled vaguely on my abdomen, the other raised and moving as if I were shining the air.